To Cheryl,
may your breath
give you the stories
that need to light —

slote,
Birdie Dawn

In Praise of Brenda Kwon's
The SUM of BREATHING

The Sum of Breathing is moving because of its honesty, and beautiful because of its exquisite writing. Somewhere near its center are the convoluted feelings about visiting the land of a grandfather she never knew, when alienation spills over into family and romantic relationships.

> —**Elaine Kim,** Writer-director, *Slaying the Dragon Reloaded: Asian Women in Hollywood and Beyond*

The characters and voices in *The Sum of Breathing* gulp at life, at times hyperventilating on those nasty doubts only the honest will admit to—am I loved enough? pretty enough? good enough?—bravely exposing these fundamental anxieties with humor, bravado, and compassion.

> —**Cathy Song,** Winner of the Yale Series of Younger Poets Award and the Shelley Memorial Award from the Poetry Society of America

Kwon's witnessing to the power of identity is revelatory and instructive. She writes of values and practices inherent in bloodline, culture, and immigrant conflicts. She remembers, recovers, and voices life's journey from womb to tomb, through love's dancing excitement and paralyzing troubles. She transcends diversity that divides and leaves us with embers that reveal our transnational humanity. Excellent read!

> —**Kathryn Waddell Takara,** winner of the 2010 American Book Award for *Pacific Raven: Hawai'i*

In Brenda Kwon, we are given the diaphanous world that bridges the ancient homeland and the new. Her words and imagery create fresh revelations and ultimately show us the triumphs of the everyday in its jubilations and confusions. This is marvelous writing.

> —**Gary Pak,** author of *The Watcher of Waipuna, A Ricepaper Airplane, Children of the Fireland,* and *Language of the Geckos and Other Stories*

Brenda Kwon's poems mine subtle and lyrical veins, resolving contradictions and opening remarkable lines of thought. Who else could combine "mangoes" and "molten volcanoes," tease out their hidden essences, and yet link their sensuous and visceral meanings for the reader? You will better understand the kinship between nature and nurture after reading this book.

—**Russell C. Leong,** author, professor, and editor of *Amerasia Journal* (1977 – 2010)

With tongue sharp and smooth, Brenda Kwon dissects comfortable ideas of self and "home," only to reconfigure them in new and startling ways; the familiar becomes unfamiliar in this collection where the immigrant past, the diasporic present, and the geography of memory converge.

—**Nora Okja Keller,** author of *Comfort Woman* and *Fox Girl*

The SUM of BREATHING

THE
Sum
OF
Breathing

BRENDA KWON

Bamboo Ridge Press

Honolulu, Hawaiʻi

ISBN 978-0-910043-91-5

This is issue #105 (Spring 2014) of *Bamboo Ridge, Journal of Hawai'i Literature and Arts* (ISSN 0733-0308)

Published by Bamboo Ridge Press
Printed in the United States of America
Indexed in *Humanities International Complete*
Bamboo Ridge Press is a member of the Council of Literary Magazines and Presses (CLMP).
Book design: Stephanie Chang Design Ink

Bamboo Ridge Press is a nonprofit, tax-exempt corporation formed in 1978 to foster the appreciation, understanding, and creation of literary, visual, or performing arts by, for, or about Hawai'i's people. This publication was made possible with support from the National Endowment for the Arts (NEA) and the Hawai'i State Foundation on Culture and the Arts (SFCA), through appropriations from the Legislature of the State of Hawai'i (and grants by the NEA).

ART WORKS.
arts.gov

HAWAI'I
STATE FOUNDATION on
CULTURE and the ARTS

Bamboo Ridge is published twice a year. For subscription information, back issues, or a catalog, please contact:
Bamboo Ridge Press
P.O. Box 61781
Honolulu, HI 96839-1781
808.626.1481
brinfo@bambooridge.com
www.bambooridge.com

5 4 3 2 1   14 15 16 17 18

for King-Kok and Alex

Table of Contents

There is one way of breathing that is shameful and suffocating.
Then, there's another way: a breath of love
that takes you all the way to infinity.

~Rumi

Descending Buddha

As if the body wouldn't remember,
narrow steps teach us respect.
Never turn your back to Buddha—
so leaving this temple,
we place our feet side by side,
careful and deliberate,
descending like crabs.
On a train ride from Kyongju to Seoul,
we count small crosses like children
standing guard in the mountains,
defiant reminders of those who left.
There is no return when one finds God—
the soul moves toward what comes after.
Still, there must be some comfort in coming back.
Even now, the thought of leaving
this place of my blood becomes
a fist in my heart,
less attachment than the recognition
of the spirit mirroring itself in what surrounds.

I, too, would return if I could.
Descending from Buddha
on these slender steps,
it is impossible to lose sight of the gaze
that beckons the art of perfection,
inviting us to bloom and close and open again,
greeting each day,
lotuses on the water.

Inheritance

Among other things
I inherit her solitude; there are moments
when I, cutting
green beans into slivers, find
I have been chewing my tongue—
something I have seen her do
when alone. It is
the taste of loss and memory,
and I wonder which stories
she has yet to keep from me.
The picture I have
is her face long before us;
she does not smile though
it's her eyes that will tell you
how she felt that day
after she pulled back her hair
put on her best blouse
the matching scarf, her fingers
knotting the ends. But
for now she would stop,
her tongue at rest
in her mouth as she
anticipated the flash. You see,
she knew she was not alone.
There are words locked in
and beneath her tongue,
words I may never hear
nor understand. As I chew
my own tongue I want
it to taste to me
of words she has never said,

secrets she has kept too well,
words for which I listen carefully
in the sound of my own
breath.

Flight

She once caught an avocado between her hands.
Poised on a rock beneath the tree in our backyard,
she leapt, seizing alligator-green
then landed tender in the grass,
no signs of sore leg or blue veins
in the way she clutched her prize to her chest
then held it out to me when she saw me watch.

I took that prize
because I know the language of a mother's care
and how she feeds to say *I love you*
but her real gift was flight,
those few seconds she lifted up,
left behind the weight of stone,
her seventy-two-year-old body slicing the air the way it did
in the decades-ago pirouettes and grand jetés
that pulsed her blood in the days before my grandmother threatened,
If you become a dancer, I will break your legs.

I have never seen her dance,
her only recital shaped by the ballerina who pas de bourrées
in my head with a choreography composed of fragments:
the lift of her arms pinning sheets to the line,
the point of her toe when she steps on the gas,
the tilt of her chin as she tucks the phone between shoulder and ear,
her stage the story of our lives,
whirling through piano lessons, band practice, basketball, and hula,
three meals per day and reminders to sleep,
her music the waltzes I hear her hum when she is dreaming of the girl
she never stopped being.

Maybe that's why she tied me to pink leather slippers,
stitching elastic to hold my girl-feet in,
combed my hair back so it wouldn't fall as I spin,
my child's body the artist she could never become.
Insisting I learn how to rise above ground,
she watched me graduate from the balls of my feet
to the tips of my toes
'til the only things holding me down to the earth
were wood and a millimeter's thickness of satin
because she believed if I only kept going,
chassé, arabesque, sauté, elevé
I would lift off the ground and learn how to fly.

And so I danced in satin, ribbons, and wool,
but flew in sound, letters, and words,
and the day I untied those ribbons forever
was the day she let go of dreams
that puppeted me across the floor,
me,
the girl her womb the dance she carried inside,
stirring long after the laces fell unbound,
the cord that tied us clipped and cut.

So she packed away my winged feet
but refused to break my fingers' flight
over the lined platform of clean white pages.
And she followed me through my many stages,
her steps en avant
soon syncopated
by swollen leg and tilted hips, unjustly weighted,
while my pen would glissade loops, crosses, and points,
each piece choreographed by the permission to dance.

But beneath my lyrics I would always hear
her earthbound rhythm, that supporting beat,
too, the pauses that grew between each step
in what I imagined was flight but knew was time,
silvering her hair, curving her back, measuring her sleep,
slowing her breath.
And in those silences I recalled that leap,
her body supported by her memory of flying,
knowing that when the time comes for her to dance,
there will be no stones to break her fall.

Mango Seed

i.
For company,
we slice mangos in the kitchen,
peel soft yellow-green skin into strips
as juice runs down our hands.
On a clean white plate,
chunks of orange-yellow meat,
three silver forks with three paper napkins
for the guests.
We nibble with care,
dabbing streams from our mouths
between exchanges and chatter
while in the kitchen the mango seeds wait alone
to be devoured over the sink,
sticky liquid down forearms,
strings in our teeth,
as we scrape, scrape, pull the meat from the core.
Seeds are for privacy,
a secret indulgence.

ii.
Next to foil-wrapped kalbi and
kong namul in a Ziploc,
she places two mangos
nestled in newspaper.
They are small and green,
tough like rocks,
two angry eggs, clenched like fists.
Mangos here on the mainland are so expensive.
Hard to believe we used to get
so many for free.

My years in L.A.
have made me hard.
I imagine my heart like molten rock,
bright fire poking beneath
the porous black surface
always threatening, waiting
to turn into stone.

iii.
On her way out, my mother pats my cheek,
tells me not to study too much.
For one moment
we stand quiet in the doorway,
thinking of things we have left behind.
From down the hallway, she calls,
The seed is the best part,
as if she smells
the tough, green scent
of angry mangos waiting to ripen.

The Wake

I didn't want to see the body. Had I known that my grandmother would be lying there on the table as if she were waiting to be dissected, I would've refused to go. My mother's grief had worsened her already selective disregard for details, and she'd never mentioned exactly what it meant that we were meeting the family for the viewing. Nor did I ask. My fear of my mother's sadness kept my questions locked inside. I didn't want to add to her burden.

I'd seen my mother sad many times. When I was young, she would quietly rock herself, whispering, "aigu jukda"—*I want to die*—in a way that always made me feel that she would disappear if I only blinked my eyes, and so I would stare at her, fixing her with my gaze as if I could chain her to me. I never knew why she said this, though I sensed it had something to do with the fact that I had no father, and like all small children who don't understand their parents' pain, I thought I was at fault, and so I learned not to speak in those moments, only to watch her, ready at a moment's notice to grasp her and haul her back should she try to leave.

But this grief was different. She spoke. She spoke to keep silence from fertilizing her suffering. She had lost her mother, the person she had known longest in her lifetime, and the absence left a void she filled with words. It was her way of showing that my grandmother's dying wouldn't pull her across what she perceived as the fragile membrane between life and death. It was as if she were dancing delicately on the border wobbling beneath her feet.

"I wonder if Auntie Grace knows that the caterers are coming a half-hour earlier tomorrow morning." She wasn't asking me the question, but I answered her anyway.

"We can find out when we get to the funeral parlor."

My mother signaled to change lanes, turning her head to check her blind spot, as she taught me to do when I was learning to drive. Her light blue dress contrasted with the pale cream of her skin. She had her tongue out, folded over her top lip.

"Sharon's supposed to bring the box for the envelopes, too. She'd better not wrap it in something bright. White is better."

"I can do it, if you want." My cousin Sharon, from my dad's side, had just had her second child, and I figured wrapping-paper colors were low on her list of priorities.

"This light is so long."

The back of my blouse began to feel damp. I didn't know what to wear, and as usual, when I felt unsure, I overdressed. The weight of my lined skirt pressed on my thighs like a blanket, the cuffs of my sleeves brushing my wrists. I knew that white was reserved for the day of the funeral, but I didn't know if there was a traditional color for a viewing. I rolled up the windows and switched on the air conditioning. The cool air surprised my mother, and she turned to look at me.

"Who told you to wear grey?"

I didn't bother to answer her.

When we pulled into the parking lot, I could see from the cars that my auntie and uncle and cousins were already there. My mother was never late; she always arrived fifteen to twenty minutes early for everything, so I didn't understand why we seemed to be last.

"The parking lot needs to be repaved. There's Auntie Grace's car."

She stepped out and moved quickly towards the double doors of the funeral parlor, barely giving me enough time to close the door before I heard the locks shut heavily, metal pulling into itself.

The parlor was next to the canal, which smelled like sulfur and was littered with trash. A few egrets picked through decaying milk cartons jutting out from the dull mud left behind by the evaporating water. I wondered if there really were any fish or bugs left in those milky pools, or if the poking motion of those birds' beaks was the habit of survival.

By the time I'd walked around the car, my mother was already through the double-doors of the building, a thinly-disguised warehouse that had been converted into a funeral home. The beige paint reminded me of the old gymnasium at my elementary school, and for a moment, I imagined that inside I would find small children playing dodgeball with the red rubber balls we used in P.E. As I walked in, a blast of cold air greeted me, making me glad I'd dressed heavily. I heard voices down the hall and to the right and hurried toward them.

I saw her before I could stop. As I rounded the corner, I glimpsed, through the open door of one of the rooms, my grandmother's body on a platform, half-covered with a blanket. My right foot planted hard, refusing to move forward. She was only a blur of dull flesh to me before I spun around and ran down the hallway, back towards the doors.

I fled outside, out of the cold, away from the pale blue carpets and vanilla walls, away from the color of dead flesh. I tried to shove the sight of my grandmother out of my head, but I could only recall the flat grey of her skin, the cream-colored blanket, then the black hair of heads bowing down, someone's purple blouse, the shiny tan metal of the chair backs. A brown jacket. I tried to swirl the colors in my head so that they would blend and become an indistinguishable mess, but they stayed in their positions, painting the memory I knew would never leave me.

I ran out to the canal because there was nowhere else to go. The egrets were still picking at the cartons, oblivious. I couldn't sit in the car because I didn't have the keys. Nothing else but a tire factory and a television studio was nearby. I sank to the ground and closed my eyes, feeling the warm, rocky pavement below me.

No one came to get me.

I knew my mother wouldn't ask me about what happened because she had her own pain to swallow. But mine needed somewhere to go. Unlike her, I couldn't chatter mine away. Mine didn't want to come out as small staccato phrases about trivial things. Mine needed to burst outward like an anchored rope thrown towards the magical groove in a rock that would secure me, help me crawl forward. But I knew if I threw it towards my mother, she would let it drop at her feet and I would fall.

She said nothing to me when she found me sitting on the trunk of the car, my legs dangling over the edge, kicking the bumper with the backs of my heels. She unlocked the doors, got inside, and started the car. I said nothing as I slid off the back, adjusted my shoes, and got in. We were the last ones to arrive and the first to leave. In the passenger side mirror, I saw my cousins walk out of the building and stop, watching our car pull out of the parking lot.

"Tomorrow morning, you better take your own car in case you have to do some errands at the funeral."

I glanced at her. Her lips were still, as if she had said nothing at all. Her eyes were fixed straight ahead, but I knew she could see me watching her.

"Did you hear me, Sara? I said you better take your own car."

I turned to watch the man in the car next to us. He hunched forward over the wheel, his back the curve of a turtle's shell.

"Sara."

I kept my head turned.

"Did you hear me?"

I had been indulging her with inconsequential responses since the day after she came home from the hospital and told me my grandmother had died. It had been a way to accommodate her, to give her a script to help her fill the silences. But I didn't feel like running lines.

She exhaled tightly, the way she did when she was trying to control her anger. I wasn't looking at her, but I knew she was gripping the wheel. For a moment I thought maybe I'd gone too far.

I didn't know what her response would be. I learned early never to challenge my mother beyond the point of acceptable childhood rebelliousness. I never thought of her striking me as abuse. I knew her lesson even then, that she was teaching me to gauge when I was in danger—not only with her, but with anyone.

But this was different. My grandmother had just died. The rules had to change. She had never once asked me if I was okay, never once tried to comfort me.

I waited, feeling the silence thicken, pushing against our bodies and the windows of the car. My heart began beating hard. I wanted the explosion. I held my breath.

Her voice was soft and sharp.

"You better do it."

When we got home, she got out of the car so quickly that she locked me in.

My mother had brought home-cooked meals to my grandmother at the care home four times per week. It seemed that she was constantly preparing, shopping, cleaning, placing juk or sashimi or ginger chicken or jeon into the small Tupperware containers that had "SUYEON KIM" written on them with thick black Sharpies. As if any other daughter in that ward would have done the same and taken her containers by mistake.

I hated going to the ward. The cheery pictures drawn in crayon by visiting kindergartners and the large block-letter signs littering the walls with childish pictures and captions that said things like "Everyone Loves A Smile" were a flimsy cover-up for the abandonment and hopelessness that permeated the halls.

That day, a woman's low moan droned on like a weak siren. The nurses and aides chatted energetically among themselves, filling small white cups with medications and writing on charts. No one paid attention to the moaning, but then I realized that there really was nothing to do. The moan couldn't be fixed; it was the sound of a woman whose pain wasn't conditional but terminal.

Everyone is dying, but the old people there were so much closer and knew it.

My mother, who had a fast stride anyway, didn't break the rhythm of her steps as she scooted around a Japanese man in a wheelchair languidly propelling himself forward with one leg that swept the ground the way skateboarders do to keep their boards rolling. He looked up at her expectantly, then watched her as she turned into my grandmother's room.

"Hi," I said, as I passed him.

He looked at me, surprised. His face was mottled with age spots, but his eyes were kind. He seemed so thin. I'd never known my grandfathers, and my father died when I was an infant, so I had a soft spot for old men. In confusion, he moved his mouth a little, but no words came out. I didn't know if it was because I had said something to him or if he thought he should have known who I was and couldn't remember.

In the room, my mother removed the large black headphones my grandmother wore to listen to the news, tucking them near the pillow, then pressed the switch near the railing to prop the bed and my grandmother up. She did everything without moving her feet more than a few inches from where she had been standing. As in a well-choreographed dance, the guard rail lowered, the rolling table slid in place, and the Tupperware containers were arranged before my grandmother just as they would be in a Korean restaurant: the soup in front of her, the rice to the left, the main dish behind the soup, and the small dishes of seasoned vegetables and kimchi in a tiny semicircle arcing away from her.

"Sungnim-ssi, gomawo." She still used my mother's name, the name my mother hated because it translated to something like "do your duty." "Sara-ssi, wasseo?" She said this even though my mother gently nudged her mouth with a spoonful of rice that had been dipped in the seaweed soup.

"Ye," my mother responded, pushing the spoon a little harder.

I stood awkwardly to the side, not wanting to crowd either of them. I moved towards the small sink outside of the bathroom and leaned against it. They seemed so complete in their routine. My mother fed, my grandmother ate. I listened to the hollow sound of the metal spoon tapping the plastic containers as my mother dug into them.

"Sara-ssi, meogeosseo?" I took a step toward the bed. My mother said nothing. I knew that the question had something to do with eating, but I wasn't completely sure.

"What, Mom?"

"She wants to know if you ate."

"Tell her yeah."

"Tell her yourself."

My grandmother was blind, and I knew she heard better out of her left ear than her right, so I moved around my mother towards the head of the bed.

"Yeah, Halmeoni. I ate." She was focused on her meal. "You eat."

The room returned to the quiet sounds of my grandmother's lunch. The clanking, slurping, chewing sounds continued. Eventually, my grandmother finished her meal and let out a loud belch. I laughed, but my mother shot me a look. Then she began reaching, wiping, stacking, rolling, and within minutes, my grandmother lay back on her bed, wearing headphones as if we had never been there.

"Does she ever go outside?" I looked out the window at a small patch of sunlight on the ground below.

"Sometimes she likes to sit in the sun." She turned to my grandmother, moving part of the headphones, and said something to her in Korean. My grandmother shook her head and repositioned the headphones. "She doesn't want to go out today."

"She must get bored."

"Are you kidding? She has the news. Always news, news, news." She went to the sink and began washing her hands.

On top of the dresser, a construction-paper drawing of a cat rested against a plastic cup. The cat had been outlined with yellow yarn, its tail a thick tassel, but its face was drawn in with red crayon. Signed on the bottom corner in purple crayon was the name "Kimberly." In the upper left-hand corner, Kimberly had written "I luv you Sueyen."

My mother glanced at the large clock on the wall. She leaned over and yelled something at my grandmother, who nodded.

"Tell Halmeoni goodbye."

I touched my grandmother's hand lightly. "Halmeoni, bye."

She removed one side of her headphones and then gripped my hand. "Bye bye."

Pulling away didn't feel right, but my mother had already left, most likely halfway to the elevators by now.

"Halmeoni. Okay?" I didn't know what I was asking her, so when she tilted her head a little, I said, "You okay? Okay?"

"Okay," she said. Then she patted my hand and waved me out.

As I left, I said goodbye to the old man, now propelling himself in the other direction down the hall. He looked at me briefly, then continued his motion forward.

I broke into a trot to catch up with my mother. It took me a few seconds to realize the moaning woman had become quiet. For a moment, I thought in horror that maybe she had died, but then it began again, an achy groan winding up slowly into a sad, weak alarm.

The next night, my grandmother died. I had been reading *Dubliners* for English class when the phone rang. In retrospect, I remember that my mother's voice seemed more clipped than usual, that she walked out the door without her keys and had to come back for them, that she was gone for a few hours. When she came home, I was watching a documentary about wolves.

The door opened and I heard her toss her keys into the drawer in the kitchen where she always kept them. She walked in between me and the television, then into her bedroom, closing the door. I got up and went to her room, knocking softly on the door.

"Mom?"

There was no answer.

"Mom, are you okay? Is everything okay?" I gripped the doorknob, knowing that none of the bedroom doors had locks on them, but I didn't go in even though I wanted to see her, know that she was just changing for bed or maybe making a phone call to the childhood friends from Korea she still kept in touch with. But there was no sound, no noise. I put my ear to the door, listening, but all I heard was the crunch of my hair as I pressed harder to listen.

"Mom?"

Finally, she answered.

"Go to sleep, Sara. Halmeoni died."

Her voice was as ordinary as if she had told me to wash the dishes.

"What—what do you mean she died?"

"Halmeoni died, Sara."

"But we just saw her yesterday." My grandmother's body had been breaking down for years, but her mind, sharp as ever, made me believe she was farther from death than she really was. "She ate so much."

"She threw it up after we left. She always throws it up."

"How long has she been doing that?"

"Go to sleep, Sara."

I began to twist the knob in my hand, mostly because I had questions, but also because I wanted to see what my mother was doing, if she was sprawled on the bed and crying silently, or slunk down on the floor against the wall, or sitting in the chair next to her bed, numb and confused. The latch made a soft shunting sound.

"I said go to bed." There was something in her voice that was cold, hard.

I backed away a few steps, fixed on the wood grains before me and the silence that thickened the door between us.

At the funeral, people honored my grandmother's remains, kept in a small brass vase placed on an altar next to the picture of her when she was young, maybe in her twenties. My mother and I had brought separate cars, but I had no errands to do, no emergencies thrown my way. We didn't interact. My mother floated from one guest to the next, talking and talking, even laughing here and there. Almost everyone wore white. My mother, in her white linen tunic, was easy to lose in the crowd of bodies milling in the hall.

Except for a few phrases, the minister from my grandmother's church spoke entirely in Korean. I bowed my head with the others, stood when everyone else did, and sang "Amazing Grace" softly in English while operatic tones belted forward from random members of the church choir. I had been assigned no duties—my cousin Sharon continued to watch over the envelopes and signatures in the guest book while her husband, John, kept an eye on their kids. My other cousin James and my Uncle Gilbert directed people to the room next door for Korean food. Auntie Grace was setting up the tables and plasticware. I didn't know what to do with myself. I didn't feel like helping anyone. I didn't want to be there, but I couldn't leave, either.

The room emptied quickly as everyone shuffled into the next room for lunch. Eventually, only my grandmother and I were left in the hall. I sat in one of the chairs near the back, staring at the black and white photo of my grandmother. I could make out the round shape of her face and the printed scarf around her neck. People used to tell me that when I was a baby, I looked just like my grandmother with her full cheeks and squinting smile.

I felt a hand on my shoulder.

"Sara." It was Auntie Grace. "You not going eat?"

I glanced away from her and out the door toward the voices coming from the hall.

"I'm not hungry."

"There's a lot of food," she said, coaxing.

The smell of sesame oil, shoyu, and beef floated in from the catering trays.

"I don't feel like it."

She stood over me, the hem of her white holoku brushing my feet. She patted my shoulder softly.

"You wanna just stay here then?"

I wanted her to sit with me, but I knew they needed her in the other room.

"Yeah. I'm okay."

Sometimes, being with her seemed like being with my dad, even though I had never known him. She was his sister, and she felt like my connection to him.

Auntie Grace tucked my hair behind my ear.

"You know, kiddo, it's not easy, yeah? For your mom."

That's what everyone had been saying to me.

"I know."

"Your mom, she was the only one who took care of your grandma."

"I know."

"And now she doesn't have a mother. So it's hard. Not easy losing your mother, you know?"

I didn't answer her right away.

"I know."

She smoothed my hair then turned to go.

"If you get hungry, come in, okay? After everyone leaves, we're taking Uncle Gilbert's car and your mom's car to Kuilima. The kids going stay with Auntie Barbara." She never got used to saying "Turtle Bay."

She pulled away, her white figure moving slowly farther and farther away from me, disappearing into the sounds and talk from the other room.

I turned to look at my grandmother's photo again. I wouldn't have recognized the woman looking out from behind the glass. By the time I knew her, the face in the picture had long been gone.

I had only seen ashes being scattered in the movies. I thought we would take the brass urn from the funeral, open its lid, and shake it up and down over the water, where the wind would sweep up my grandmother's remains and float them off into the distance. Instead, Auntie Grace took a thick plastic bag from a small paper one in her purse. The ashes were dark grey and looked wet. My mother stepped forward first, dipping her hand into the bag, then holding her fist out over the water as she stood perched on the edge of the rocks. She didn't linger, just turned her closed palm downward, opening her fingers and releasing what was there. After she stepped back, one by one my cousins, then my uncle, took their turns. Only Auntie Grace and I were left.

I couldn't figure out why the ashes seemed so dense. There were a few bone fragments, which I didn't expect, and my hand jerked back as my fingers grazed the shards, knocking the bag a little. Some of the ash fell on the rocks.

Auntie Grace adjusted her grip on the bag and I reached in again. The ashes were cold, like damp sand, and gritty. I took a large pinch and dropped them into the waves below. I waited to feel some kind of goodbye, a sense of something momentous, but there was nothing. I just wanted to go home.

Without thinking, I dusted my hand on my dress, leaving a dark grey smudge near my thigh. Horrified, I started to brush at it frantically. My frenzied movements caught the others' attention.

"Sara, stop it!" My mother walked awkwardly toward me, stepping over crags in the rocks.

The harder I brushed, the more it seemed the ashes were ground into the fabric.

My mother gripped my hand. "Sara. Stop!"

"Let me go!" I wrenched away from her and started shaking out my skirt.

"I said, stop it!" She reached for my wrists. We began to struggle, teetering on the rocks. Auntie Grace and Uncle Gilbert made their way toward us. Someone grabbed me around my waist. It seemed like hands were all over me. I began feeling suffocated. And then, I began screaming.

"How could you? How could you not tell me?"

"What's the matter, Sara?" It was Auntie Grace's voice.

"What's wrong?"

"How could you not tell me?" I began to cry so hard that I didn't care if my mother answered.

"How could you not tell me?" I asked over and over again, sick of holding the question in. It burst out of me, like an echo of each time I had thought it.

"Why didn't you tell me she was going to be like that? Why didn't you tell me she was going to be out like that before they burned her? Why didn't you tell me?" The hands around my waist tightened their grip. "You never told me she was going to be lying there! You could've told me! You could have told me! You don't care! You don't care about me! I didn't want to see her dead, Mom! I didn't want to see her like that!"

All I could hear was the sound of my voice, the sound of my own crying. Then suddenly, I realized my arms were free. I wiped my eyes with my forearm. I didn't have my balance on the rocks and stumbled to find my footing. I hated the feel of the sharp points under my soles. I wanted to run back to the car and leave everyone there. I was tired of the pressure to act as if I were fine. I was sick of it, sick of her, sick of everything. And that's when I heard her voice.

"I didn't either, Sara."

My sobs froze in my throat. I lifted my gaze, and for a moment, my eyes met my mother's. It felt like it had been a long time since we looked each other in the eye.

And then she began to cry. Water ran down her cheeks and over her neck, trailing onto her dress. I didn't hear her right away because I was mesmerized by her tears.

She didn't stop. I watched Auntie Grace and Sharon run up to her, hold her as she sank down, as if her body were weighted down. I watched her face contort so hard that I couldn't recognize her. I wanted to go to her, but I could only watch, see how she was already somewhere else deep inside her grief.

My grandmother's ashes were resting near the edge of the

rocks. Auntie Grace had put them down. As my mother continued to cry, I made my way toward the plastic bag, my feet searching for bits of semi-smooth surface to step on. The bag was almost full. I looked down at the water, the white foam bubbling on the rocks below. With both hands, I turned the bag upside-down and shook it, watching ashes and bone fall into the water in one heavy mass. When they hit the surface, they pulled downward and scattered, where they submerged and disappeared.

Ashes

Perhaps it was you granting respite from the rain.

Seven days since your death,
twelve white-clad figures
move precariously over rock dividing us from the sea.
With one arm drawn in,
your son holds your ashes,
while clouds hang like bellies of cats before birth.

Beneath our feet, waves hiss and whiten.
There is too much of you to relinquish at once.
As one steps forward, another moves back
until, each in turn, we let you go.
In the cup of my palm, your sand-heavy ash
is grave with parting and fragments of bone.
Sinking into the water, you pull to the floor
where you quietly rest, undistinguished from sand.

Had some weary traveler stirred from her sleep,
lured onto the balcony by warm salted air,
she would see how we scattered in a field of black,
cleaved from each other, undetermined.
Then, how we once again gathered where stone met grass,
pausing in recognition,
as we turned toward home.

The rain never fell.

Instead, huddling its droplets in ponderous vapor,
it held its break, its dispersion of mass.

And when the storm came, it felt no regret—
the division temporary, a mere transmission
before, meeting the sea,
it became whole again.

Mother Tongue

I listen to photographs.

For most people, the image is visual. They witness how the camera seizes moments violently, wresting them from oblivion or memory, or whispers secrets about small instants otherwise lost during the blink of an eye. Then there are the poses, anticipated and rehearsed, nevertheless betraying their subjects. You stand together, position your lips just right, perhaps squint slightly to avoid looking shocked when the flash goes off. You do your best to control the impression, you freeze yourself before the camera does it for you, but it never works. Look closely at any picture and you see behind the façade: *Do I look fat? Why am I always at the end? Does he still love me?*

There are voices in every image.

It's not the old woman asleep on the bus so much as it is the *clunk-whirr* of the bus propelling itself forward, the squeak of the brakes as the bus lurches to a stop, the hiss of the door as it opens, even the smallest hint of a snore when the woman exhales. It's the tinny treble of the music coming from the Walkman of the boy sitting behind her, the one who gazes out the window. It's his sigh.

And it's not the man leaning over to talk to the woman next to him, but the sound of her wine glass as she sets it down on the café table, the reverberations of its clink muted by the gloved hand that holds it, the gentle vibrating *hmm?* of her response, almost buried by the sound of Paris traffic behind her, the rumbling motors nevertheless failing to hide the scrape of his chair leg against the pavement as he moves closer to her, a louder version of the whisk of his tweed sleeve grazing the tabletop.

I pore this way over photos, listening. I let people think I really want to see snapshots of their trips to Disneyland, their weekends in Hale'iwa. No one knows I listen. Whenever I resist having my picture taken, they never suspect that I'm afraid that someone will see my picture and know everything I hold inside, the secrets not yet ready for confession.

Instead, they call me shy.

It's easier this way, to let their words drape over me, *such a quiet girl, so serious,* their speech falling on me like a cool sheet, wrapping me in my world of sounds, in that world of confidences and secrets, where if I only listen, voices grow from what seems to be silent.

X✗X

The newspaper crinkles in her grasp as she hugs it tight to her body. As she shifts her weight, the smooth sheets brush against her bare arm, a light hushing sound that she would have noticed had she not been waiting for her next task. "Omma," she begins to ask—the click of the shutter—"mwohae?" Her high girl's voice is slightly scratchy at the beginning of her sentences, the way a well-rosined bow first aches a note from the violin string it has gripped below. Water drips from the wet clothes hung over the basin behind her, the steady tapping erasing itself from her attention with each predictable drop. Her mother is beyond the frame. The girl sways back and forth, her legs the clapper of the bell of worn cloth of her skirt, each movement singing the brush of fabric against skin on a hot summer day after the bombs fell.

The girl is not my mother, nor anyone she knew. The man behind the camera is no one she'd ever met. But somewhere, in an invisible radius from this moment, my mother is a fifteen-year-old girl, not yet having any idea that nine years later, she will marry my father, move to another country, her home a chain of islands in the middle of the ocean that hug her birthplace, though when she settles, she will feel that there is nothing that connects the two places. She will not see how a body of water this large links, only that it separates. And having seen division upon division–her country, how she leaves her family–it will not occur to her to have two tongues.

So she will choose one.

Like a good daughter, a good wife, a good American, she will raise her child with her Western tongue.

"Such a good mother," they will tell her. "Your daughter will be smart, go to private school."

She will forget her first tongue enough that she will eventually stumble over it. But she can never let it go because it has colored her blood for too many years. Sometimes she will want to say things to her daughter, but the new words won't always work. She will think furiously how to translate what she wants to say, but nothing will feel right. She will begin to speak, but never finish. She will feel, for decades upon decades, that she is caught mid-sentence.

Later, when her daughter grows, shows a love of the adopted words, she will accuse her child of using them unfairly, a native speaker's advantage over her own forked tongue. How can half ever beat a whole?

But she won't have understood that even her daughter's tongue is forked; one side strong, dominant, like the muscles of a leg that compensates for its amputated twin. Each powerful movement atrophies the other, and even in the most eloquent moments, her daughter feels crippled.

She'll refuse to see. Her daughter has one strong tongue. She possesses two weak ones. This is evolution, she thinks. My daughter will be more than I. My daughter will take these words and bend them like hot glass, fashion them into whatever she wants, whatever she pleases. My daughter will say all the things I never could.

Omma, mwohae?

✗✗✗

Her hair is fine because she thinks too much.

Sometimes I look at her and see the ocean in her head, her thinking like so many waves. She is lucky, I told her. I always wanted to live in another country. She says I do, but that's not what I mean.

She thinks she is going to be all alone, but she doesn't know how many people are waiting for her.

She worries enough for this whole family.

When Mina was a baby, she almost never cried. She would look at Harry and me, and we knew if she was unhappy, or happy, or hungry, just by watching her. We thought maybe something was wrong with her because she didn't talk much, but the doctor said she was okay, nothing wrong. She didn't like using her voice, but she would do other things, scrunch her fists together, scratch her head, squeeze her eyes shut, and we learned how to tell what she wanted. We had to watch her all the time. One time, when she was playing with the neighbors, she stopped just like that and then sat in the corner. I went over to her and when I touched her, her skin was burning hot with fever.

"Why didn't you say you felt sick," I scolded her, pushing her out toward the garage so I could drive us home.

But she just leaned against me with her eyes closed.

I have to watch her to see what she needs, since she won't say.

For one month, Mina's been making a pile of things to take to Korea. She has boxes of tampons, bottles of shampoo, her makeup, all of the brands she thinks she can't get there.

"Seoul is modern," I told her. "They have almost everything."

She just made the pile bigger with vitamins, hairspray, lotion, laundry detergent.

"Where are your books?" I asked. "The school isn't going to care how good you look if you don't have books." Every day until she left, she added something else.

Mina makes me scared with all her packing, like she is getting ready for war. Each thing she takes means she has to go outside one less time, talk to people she doesn't know, ask questions. The pile is like a fort for her. She thinks it shows her preparation, but it doesn't. It grows, just like her fear.

I told her, "When you have children, you will understand.

When they're happy, you're happy. When they're sad, you will feel sad. When you worry, I worry too. You have Auntie Eun-Young and Auntie Moonsu, and Auntie So-Hee said she would drive from Busan to see you. They are all waiting for you. My friends will take care of you."

But Mina still thinks she will be alone.

She doesn't know I see how she talks all the time, inside her head. Sometimes I say, "The words gotta come out," and she looks at me like she doesn't know what I mean.

I want to tell her, "You are always alone anyway, always inside your head so much. In Korea, it's same thing. What's the difference?"

But still, she worries.

Months before I decided to go to Korea, my mother wanted me to watch the soap operas that chained her to her television every night at 8:00, 7:00 on Sundays. It only got worse when I had my ticket in hand.

"This is a good way for you to learn about Koreans. The stories are so real—just like real life! Too, they have subtitles, so you can tell what they're saying. The one right now, so true. This girl, her husband's mother thinks she's not good enough, and so they fight, and the mother, she blames the girl for everything..."

"Mom, I don't need to learn how to say, 'How could my son marry you!' or 'I'm going to kill myself!' I need to get around."

"You will. Don't worry so much. But the shows can teach you what Koreans are like. At UH, there was a big thing. All these professors came to talk about them," she said, vindicated.

Whenever she started in on the dramas, I let her talk for awhile and then changed the subject by asking her some practical question, like whether it would be a good idea to take my cold remedies with me or just buy them in Seoul, even though I knew that American products were a luxury item in Korea and that unless I wanted to pay almost double, I had better make a trip to the drugstore. But sooner or later, she'd be back on the subject. I stopped answering her phone calls at 7:59 to tell me to turn on my television.

Once, when she came over to give me some boxes of dark chocolate to take to her friends in Seoul, she took a stack of DVDs out of a plastic grocery bag dangling from her wrist.

"Here, I brought these. This is a good one. This boy and this girl, they think they're brother and sister, but when his sister was born, she got switched. He likes the girl and she likes him, but even though they're not related, they feel bad about falling in love."

She sat down, popped in the disc, then worked her way through the menus until the show began. She gazed intently, absorbed by the screen even though she knew what was going to happen.

A soft focus shot of a man holding a boy stretched over the screen. As he spoke to his son, words flashed on the bottom. *That's your sister, isn't she pretty?*

"This is just the beginning," she said impatiently, squinting at my remote control to skip ahead. I never got over my surprise at how adept she was with electronic devices. While her friends struggled with email and cell phones, my mother figured out how to text me, especially when she knew I was busy and wouldn't pick up.

Suddenly distracted by the sound of wailing, I turned to see a girl, her round, pale face contorted by sobbing. Her dark hair was pulled back into a ponytail that strained the skin by her temples, and her mouth formed an uneven oval. Over and over, she cried, *Omma, Omma, Omma,* and at the bottom of the screen, in yellow letters, were the words, *Mother, Mother, Mother!*

I started to make a joke about how I already knew what "Omma" meant so I didn't need a soap opera language lesson, but the sight of my mother stopped me. She was chewing the inside of her cheeks, something she did when she was concentrating. I could almost hear the clink of her teeth, the dull crunch and rip of flesh tearing away in her mouth.

I turned back to the television. The girl was now in the background, with a woman crumpling to the ground before her. As the woman sank in tears, so did the girl, their faces mirrors of each other.

"Mom," I began.

But when I looked at her fixed on the scene before her, I knew she wouldn't hear me.

"Why do your folks like the dramas so much?" I once asked Val, whose Chinese parents became so addicted that they often ordered entire series, with Cantonese subtitles, online.

"Well, they think Koreans are really good-looking, and the stories are tragic. God, it's insane. I can't stand being around when they watch. They start yelling at the TV."

"Everybody watches them like it's crack. Maybe it's... cathartic? Like the characters do, say, and feel what no one else feels comfortable doing, saying, or feeling," I suggested.

"Yeah. My mom thinks Bae Yong Joon is hot. She has a keychain with his face on it," Val said.

When I decided to go to Korea, it was as if the only way people could relate to me was by talking about the shows.

"Oh, I love Winter Sonata! Bae Yong Joon is so handsome! Are you going to go to that Namiseom Island where they filmed it?"

"No, I'm going to Seoul."

"Oh, well you should ask people about the actors. Maybe they know where they hang out!"

Other times, I'd get a dreamy response of, "Korean women are the most beautiful women. I could watch those shows all day."

At moments like these, I wanted to spit out plastic surgery statistics, talk about how it was a rite of passage for Korean teenagers to get their eyelids done, mention that plastic surgery in Korea was the most advanced in the world. I wanted to tell them that the men and women they all thought were so beautiful had manufactured their looks, were carved-up victims of a Westernized beauty standard. I wanted to say Korean idols were chewed up and spat out as fast possible, but instead, I would smile, say I should really start watching the shows, and then let the conversation drop.

When I was a kid, no one really liked Koreans. One of my best friends, who was Japanese, never had me over to her house because her mother thought Koreans were dirty. Maybe things had been changing all along, but I couldn't get used to what seemed like an overnight obsession with Korea, what my friends and I called yobophilia. Suddenly, everyone wanted to eat Korean food, learn how to speak the language, travel to Seoul. At the Korean film festivals, there were more locals than Koreans. At Daiei, the small video store inside sold calendars, keychains, coffee mugs, all imprinted with the faces of the latest stars. Tour companies offered trips to Korea so that visitors could see the places where their favorite series were filmed.

It was so different from the Korea I learned, the Korea I carried with me—my mother having to speak Japanese in school, shamans dancing in white, the three million Koreans who died during the Korean War, my grandfather, abducted and killed by Japanese policemen.

I wasn't sure what I was looking for. I had gone there once before, five years ago, on a two-day stopover to Bangkok. I loved walking through temples and palaces, seeing the paintings, the cultural villages, things that I claimed as my own. I bought brush paintings of horses, celadon cups, a hanbok. It didn't feel like consuming. It seemed like reclaiming. The two days didn't feel like enough, but still, I hadn't thought of staying longer.

This time, one week before my departure, I started having dreams. In them, my bags were packed and everyone would be waiting for me to lock up and get in the car. I would be standing at the entrance to my apartment, refusing to leave. My arms would be braced against the doorframe. I would be trying to say I didn't want to go, but no words would come out of my mouth.

I wasn't used to having such obvious dreams, dreams I didn't have to work at. The thought of being in another country whose language I didn't speak terrified me.

My mother knew this, which is why she began pushing the dramas on me. She kept insisting I would be fine, as if speaking Korean were a dormant characteristic just waiting for the right conditions to burst out and mature. She had never spoken Korean to me unless she was upset, but I could sometimes tell by the tone of her voice what she was saying. The words themselves were empty and always had been.

She didn't understand why I was having anxiety dreams.

"Stop worrying so much. Lots of people go to Korea and not all of them speak Korean. Why are you so scared?"

"You know how to speak Korean," I retorted. "You wouldn't be afraid of going because you know how to tell them you're lost, that you need a doctor, that you're looking for the subway station. All I know how to say is 'hello,' 'yes,' 'no,' 'rice,' and 'thank you.' And 'mother.'"

She'd been so dismissive all along, like she thought it would be as easy for me to go to Korea as it would be for her. It's like she had forgotten Korea was her home once, that Korean was her first language, and that it had never been my home, my tongue.

She had looked at me with a furrow in her brow. It took me a few seconds to realize that she was surprised. But a moment later, she said confidently, "Koreans will understand you if you speak slowly, show them what you mean. These days, it's different. Not like before."

The furrow disappeared back into her skin, like a pebble sinking in water.

✗ʏ✗

Whenever Harry used to tease me about my f's, I wanted to hit him. What did he know about speaking another language? He grew up in this place, never needing anything else.

"Honey, da 'telepone' stay for you," he'd say whenever I got a call.

He didn't know I used to laugh because I was embarrassed, not because he was funny.

When he talked to his friends, he used so much pidgin, "Wat, you like one nadda one?" or "Try give 'em."

"My English is better than yours!" I once yelled at him after he'd made fun of my accent. But whenever I got mad, he called me a "yobo wahine," saying, "Das da yobo wahine temper." It was always joke, joke, joke for him.

"Do you make fun of your mother too?" I used to ask him. She had a Busan accent whether she spoke English or Korean. I barely understood her sometimes. I wondered how Harry and his brothers did. Their Korean was terrible.

Harry was dark, strong, a little loud, maybe someone I wouldn't have liked in Korea. But in Hawai'i, he fit. He looked like everyone else. He wore rubber slippers, dragged his feet when he walked. On weekends and when he came home from work, he threw his aloha shirt and pants into the hamper and put on shorts and a T-shirt. When we went out, he poured his beer into a glass of ice. Sometimes I doubted people would ever guess he was Korean. Even with his last name, Chun, people thought he was Chinese. To everyone, he was local.

He knew I didn't like when he spoke pidgin, especially around Mina. He even used to knock on my stomach when I was pregnant and say, "Eh, small baby, dis yo daddy. You need one pillow in dere?" just to irritate me. But then I would hear him talking to his workers. His voice was haole.

"How come you don't talk that way all the time?" I asked him. "You sound important. Respectable."

"Nah, das for work. Da guys, dey gotta know who's da boss, you know what I mean? But heah, you know I da boss, so no need!"

Always joking, my Harry.

When I was pregnant with Mina, I would sing to her. Having her in my belly made me miss home, my mother. I would tell her stories in Korean, wanting her to hear what it was like since she wasn't there. I told her the story my mother used to tell me.

A long time ago, a frog lived with his mother. He would never do what she asked. If she told him to go right, he would go left. If she told him to wake up, he would go to sleep. Each day, she wondered what to do with her son who would never listen to her.

One day, she knew that it was time for her to die, and she wanted to be buried in the mountains. But knowing her son, she told him she wanted to be buried by the river instead.

"Son," she said, "I am going to die soon."

The frog began to cry. He was very sad.

"Son," she told him, "I have one last wish."

"Yes, Mother," the frog said. "Anything you want."

"You must bury me near the river. You must not bury me in the mountain. I only want to be near the river. Do you promise?"

The frog looked at his old and dying mother and said he would do as she wished.

When she died, the frog cried and cried.

"I have been a bad son," he wept. "My whole life, I have never done as you asked. Mother, this last time I will listen to you."

That day, he buried her in sand next to the river. He was happy that he had for once done what she wanted. But that night, it began to rain. The frog sat helpless, watching the river rise. Soon, the river overflowed and washed his mother's grave away. The frog, terrified and in despair, sat near the water and sobbed as he watched his mother float away.

And this is why frogs always croak next to the river and especially when it rains.

It was a story all Korean mothers told their children.

"Mina," I would whisper her as I carried her in my stomach, "you should always listen to me. Don't be like the frog and cry your whole life because you didn't."

When it was time for me to give birth, so much water gushed out of me. Mina wasn't any trouble, just slipped right out into the doctor's hands. If it wasn't for the cord, maybe she would have slipped away. She looked so much like Harry that he couldn't stop laughing when he first held her. "Das my baby girl," he said proudly, giggling like a child.

The nurses called her a princess because she had so much hair when she was born, and long eyelashes, too. She was pretty even though most babies are red and wrinkled. They liked her because she didn't cry and didn't fuss when they held her.

"What a perfect little girl," they all told me.

That afternoon, as I was resting at the hospital, I remember looking out my window at the ocean, how blue it was. I thought of how I crossed all that water and came here.

I held Mina in my arms, watching her tiny fingers open and close. *We are both travelers*, I thought. *I wonder if she will leave her birthplace like I did.* I looked out at the water again, how peaceful it was with the sun shining, the boats bobbing in the basin.

When I looked at her sleeping, I saw a little Harry in my arms. Like Harry, she belonged here. She wasn't dark like the sun made him, but she had his wide-set eyes, his lips, the lower one curved like a bow. She looked so comfortable in my arms, even though she spent so many months inside. Her chest moved up and down fast, breathing so much air.

In my head, I had the words of the song I used to hear my mother chant to me to make me sleep, *jal ja, jal ja, jal ja*.

"Mina," I whispered as I rocked her back and forth, "sleep good, sleep good, sleep good."

Idiom

-for Nancy

And then she is laughing
having misspoken an idiom:
Get on your ball
though this makes sense to me.
I imagine the taming
involved in discipline,
something that feels like
a bear on a ball,
balanced and delicate
for fear of a whip—
sometimes I hear how
she speaks like my mother,
whose language is framed
by too many borders
and then not enough. Between
dawn's early light and
the morning calm, she
dreams of her tongue, yet
for now she will tell me
her childhood is locked
in words of hangeul
she has now forgotten, though
they haunt her sometimes
when she is silent; and
hearing her voice
I watch how she stands
balancing on a treacherous surface
threatening the fall,
the crack of the whip
demanding that she indeed perform—

that she tame the wild tongue
that twists in her mouth:
to command and to master
for fear of revolt.

Aigu

She begs words from my lips, and
though I wish to tell her everything
I tell her this instead:
There is a language I wish to unlearn
because I am afraid of the words,
of what they create. I am afraid
of their sound, of the way
they sometimes refuse to obey me.
I wear them like the second-hand coat
belonging to someone else
and have clothed myself
with those awkward threads
woven together by silence.
I remember the way you used to sigh,
and how you would whisper
that word you could never
translate,
the word born
from the blood-weary depths
of ancestral pain   *aigu*
and have heard your mantra
thickening the air on
moon-filled nights   *aigu, aigu jam.*

There is too much to say,
the words a flood of sounds in my throat,
and I feel my mouth hollow,
empty,
whispering   *aigu*
the sound which tells me
this tongue is mine,
and I repeat the words   *aigu, aigu*
as if it had been there all along.

Mul

The water rippled around my chest. It tugged at my waist, pushing my thighs and wrapping around my hips. Beneath the surface, my toes clung to the sand, gripping against the current. I imagined my legs like trees, rooted deep.

So long as I was in water, we could never relax, my mother and I. I could see her in the distance, standing on the grass past the sand, her body poised and attuned to the slightest change in me, ready to rescue me from what I was convinced would pull me under. It was as if I had inherited her fear of water, but where she learned to float, I had developed an inability to submerge. As long as I stayed in the shallows, I knew I could be saved.

"You have to let go," she said later as she sat next to me on the sand. She pulled the edge of the blanket beneath us and covered my legs. The sun had begun to set and the sky's blue absorbed the grey of the coming dark. She stroked my hair away from my face, sifting through the wet strands with her fingers. "If you're afraid, you'll sink."

I leaned into her body and breathed in her warmth, the smell of the salt wind on her skin. The breeze blew in my ears like a whisper, hushing the sounds of the people around us.

"I don't want to come to the beach anymore."

Her hands stopped for a moment.

"When I met your father, I said I would move here because I thought this would feel like home." I looked up to see her gazing out at the sea. Her voice was soft, woven into the wind. "I grew up by the water, too, but I was so afraid. I wanted things to be different for you."

The sun sank beneath the horizon. I imagined the ocean extinguishing its fire, a steaming stone dropping fathoms deep. The waves hissed as they washed the sand, leaving sizzling foam in their wake.

There was a closeness to my mother's body that I craved, as if I could remember what it was like when she carried me. In her body I had floated, a thought that comforted me. Staying near her side, I felt protected. Especially since my father had died when I was so young, she was the center of my perimeter, my patterns and motions never moving me farther than she could reach.

"I used to sing to you," she'd tell me, placing her hands on her belly to show me the way she looked before I was born. "Korean songs and opera, so that you would be smart." Then she'd sing songs I remembered from childhood. Her music always settled my bones. I couldn't imagine a time she wouldn't be with me. When other girls began rebelling against their parents, I clung to my mother and the safety she brought.

I didn't know why the ocean scared me, why even pools seemed like mirrors of that vastness. Looking at those bodies of water, I could only see an unsteady surface, the way the depths were hidden away. I was afraid what was below would pull me in, that despite my best efforts, I would drown.

That night after we came home from beach, my mother lay beside me as I prepared for sleep, the wet floral scent of her shampooed hair enveloping us. She had never broken the habit of tucking me into bed.

"I used to be like you, Anna. But when your dad brought me here, I thought, *People here swim.* At first, he tried to teach me, but he didn't let me go too far." She laughed softly. "If I wanted to learn, I had to do it myself. So I went to the YMCA. My teacher was a pretty haole lady."

I tried to picture my father holding my mother as she floated facedown among the waves. I imagined him sliding his arms beneath her as the water took the place of his support. He must've loved her too much to let her swim away, to allow the current to steal her from him. In all the photos of the two of them, they smile as if they are keeping a secret. I wondered, if my father were alive, would he do the same with me? How far would he let me go?

"You were still scared, though."

She ran her hands over the wrinkled sheet. It was summer and too hot for blankets, so she had washed and put them all away.

"I was terrified. And I felt silly. I wouldn't let your dad come to the lessons. But I think he might have snuck in to watch me anyway. Because later, he would say, 'Haejin, did you have fun?' But he wasn't very good at lying. He tried to pretend he was really asking."

I didn't know if anyone would ever love me the way my father seemed to love her.

"You're not going to make me take lessons, right?"

"No, no. Maybe later when you're not so scared." Then she lifted herself off the bed.

"Anna-sshi," she said, "we don't have to go anymore if you don't want."

I thought of the ritual we'd always had, going to the beach the last Sunday of every month. We would take our lunches late in the afternoon and sit on the grass, talk and laugh until it was dark. We had been doing this for as long as I could remember. It was something my parents had done before my father died.

"Maybe. I don't know."

My mother stroked smooth my forehead with her thumb to wish me good dreams. "Jal ja" she said, telling me to sleep well, then patted my shoulder softly before turning out the light, closing the door behind her with a soft click.

As I lay in bed, I felt the motion of the water swaying me. I tensed myself to still the tide, but it soaked through my skin, sliding into my veins. Eventually, I fell asleep to its rhythm, a boat rocking in the pulse of my own blood.

My mother was beautiful in a way I wasn't.

In the pictures of her when she was in high school, her figure defies the heavy wool of her school uniform, her stance a dead giveaway to the hours she spent dancing. Years after motherhood changed her body, her legs were still long and lean, her training something I saw when she stood at the sink, her left leg extended, pointed toes to the floor. For as long as I could remember, she had always been elegant, gliding through her everyday gestures. She moved within the ghost of her youth, always dancing inside the ballerina.

My body was neither lithe nor limber. Everyone said I resembled my father. I sometimes hated how short I was, the broadness of my shoulders, the squareness of my hips, the swell of muscles wrapping around my bones, but my mother reminded me that these things were proof that I carried my father. She told me how he was so strong, how she married him because she knew he could do things, not like the boys in Korea who drank coffee and smoked cigarettes, discussing politics all day. She liked the way he was comfortable when he was outside.

While the girls around me began to change, their bodies softening into womanhood, my body refused, held by his echoes. At twelve, I wasn't wearing a bra, though I begged my mother to buy me one so I could at least pretend. But my jeans hung straight from my hips, needing no belt to pull loose fabric in toward my waist. While the boys stared at my budding classmates, I continued to feel as if I were a child.

It was during that time that my mother's beauty began to hurt, building a resentment in me because I couldn't draw her genes to show on the surface. I would stand before the mirror, dissecting my body, the parts I deemed unacceptable becoming enemies I despised. I would catalog what I wanted to keep, scorn the rest and wish it away, but each morning I woke up to find what I hated and accepted still connected and fused.

I had given up daring to follow in my mother's beauty, but I decided I could at least move as she did. She agreed to let me take ballet lessons, and I began spending my Saturday mornings with a woman in her fifties who seemed like a leaf floating on air.

On the way to my first class, I sat tense and nervous. I imagined a roomful of girls just like my mother who glided and twirled while I stumbled around them. My mother noticed that I'd stopped speaking and began to hum one of my favorite songs. The sound of her voice wrapped itself around me, cocooning me in low, vibrating tones.

"Anna-sshi, do you want me to go with you?"

It was a question I'd been asking myself that whole morning. I knew I'd feel better if she were there, that if I got lost, she could anchor me. A small part of me wanted to retreat into her safety. It made the risk of dancing seem less frightening.

Her hands grasped the steering wheel gently—I'd never seen her clutch it tightly—her long, pale fingers delicate in their hold. My own hands were thick, my fingers crooked. I couldn't imagine them suspended gracefully in air. I couldn't imagine any part of myself elegant and refined—only clunky and awkward, like a clumsy boy.

"No, Mom. I'm okay. Just pick me up after."

I couldn't tell if she was proud or disappointed.

After she dropped me off, I found my way into the changing room next to the studio, pulling off my shoes and slipping out of my jeans. In my bag I had packed a black leotard and pink tights, the required uniform for beginners. As I began to dress, the door slid open and another girl walked in. She was already dressed for class. Glancing around for space on the benches, she sat next to me, untying the filmy skirt around her waist. Her arms and legs were long and thin, and her hair was twisted into a dark black bun with a pink knit cover pinned into place. She watched me as I pulled on my tights.

"You're going to tear them if you grab from the waist," she said. She reached around to squeeze her bun, checking for loose pins.

"I know. I'm just adjusting them," I snapped.

She continued observing me and then sighed, pushing my hands away. "Like this." She bent down and grasped the loose fabric around my ankles, moving her hands up my leg until the tights were stretched smoothly over my thigh. "See?"

I shoved her hands away. "I was going to do that." I glanced around to see if anyone else was looking, then I imitated her movements on my other leg.

She sat back down, crossing her legs at the ankles, swinging them back and forth slowly.

"Is this your first class?"

The other girls were quietly changing. Each word she spoke echoed through the air, amplified by others' silence. Feeling as if we were on display, I wished that she would bother someone else.

"Yeah. But my mother—"

"I was taking classes before we moved here," she said. "I was almost ready to go en pointe. But they told me I had to start from the beginning. I guess Mrs. Sato is pretty picky about how she teaches."

I ignored her as I pulled on my leotard. I wondered if she was going to tell me I was doing that wrong, too.

"But Mrs. Sato is supposed to be good," she continued. "One of the best. Still, it's probably going to be easy."

I reached into my bag for my ballet slippers. The leather was cool and smooth in my hands, the suede soles soft and velvety. I almost didn't want to put them on. After my mother had sewn on the elastic, I had worn them in the house, but only when she wasn't there.

The door burst open and the girls from the previous class, all in light blue leotards, poured in. The girls in black stood quickly to make room for them, then shuffled out to the hallway and into the studio.

"I'm Julie," the girl said, following me out the door.

"Anna." I walked faster, hoping I'd lose her in the crowd.

Mrs. Sato was dressed in a navy blue leotard, pink tights, and navy blue legwarmers. Although she was tiny, her hips curved, reminding me of the graceful haunches of a deer. Every movement of hers seemed to come from a dance, and even when she walked across the floor, she lifted her chest and held her shoulders evenly.

Holding a yardstick in her hand, she called out to us and welcomed us in.

"Good morning, girls. Come in, come in. Please line yourselves up along the barre." She swept the yardstick to her right.

I was seized with a fear that we might dance one by one. I ran for a spot in the middle. Julie slid herself next to me.

"I'll go in front in case you need help," she whispered.

I didn't know why Julie had chosen me—why she thought I would need the most help. In any case, determined not to look clumsy, I focused intently on Mrs. Sato and every direction she gave.

"Ballet is the art of grace and control. To be a dancer, you must train your bodies. Face forward to the mirror, girls, your hand on the barre. Now stand like so with your backs nice and tall." Mrs. Sato demonstrated for us, regally, an invisible barre beneath her hand. Her heels touched and her feet turned out, forming a vee.

The room filled with sounds of scuffling as we took our positions. Julie's feet were turned out wide. I forced my feet further out.

"We want one long line from the tops of your heads to the backs of your heels. You can't be a dancer if your lines are weak. No protruding buttocks in this class." Mrs. Sato walked past us, occasionally tapping the yardstick on the floor, adjusting our shoulders and turning our hips.

When she got to me, she held the yardstick along my back. "One long, straight line, girls. No slouching or slanting." She nudged my hips forward with the yardstick. "Your turnout is too wide, dear." I looked at her, unsure. Her eyes were kind, but I still felt stupid. "Turn your feet in."

Reluctantly, I slid my toes closer until my knees and thighs touched.

"Good." Mrs. Sato returned to the others. "This is called 'first position.' Now hold your arms out please, nice and round. No hunched shoulders. Drop your elbows a bit." Julie's arm extended, her shoulders thrown back.

As Mrs. Sato led us through the rest of the positions; the other girls, like me, jerked as we moved from one position to the next. The piano music punctuated each missed beat. Among us, Julie glided, poised with ease. I grudgingly mirrored her, jealous of how she evoked words like "excellent," "lovely," and "beautiful" from Mrs. Sato. I had only heard "good" after fixing my feet. I wanted to hear Mrs. Sato's praise, too, and I pushed my muscles and bones until they ached. I wondered if my body would ever lengthen, if my walk would transform to a dancer's gait. I had always envisioned my mother as fluid from the very start. It didn't occur to me that it might have been something she had to learn.

When the hour ended, we lined up before the mirror. We faced our reflections, a band of black torsos and pink legs stretching across the room. I glanced at myself, quickly looking away. Even in that one moment, I saw how my legs weren't reeds, but thick turnips planted in the sockets of my hips. My fingertips stopped higher up along my legs.

"Eyes up, everyone. A dancer holds herself with pride."

We stood with our arms and legs in first position as instructed. I focused on my eyes in the mirror, ignoring everything in my periphery. We ended the class with a small bow. As soon as Mrs. Sato said, "Thank you, girls," we broke, slipping back into the routine of our bodies' habits.

Julie pranced alongside me as we moved toward the door.

"Wasn't she great?" she said, beaming. "She's so much better than my other teacher! You know she used to be a professional dancer? She even danced with the San Francisco Ballet and everything!"

As we made our way down the hall back toward the changing room, girls in dark blue leotards passing us by, someone behind us hissed the word "bitch."

It was a word with a target. I stiffened with fear. Reluctantly,

I turned around. One of the girls from our class stood there, her eyes narrowing, looking at Julie.

Julie's eyes widened. Though she said nothing, I imagined that her voice would be high, full of surprise, not confrontation.

"Think you're so good? Fucking bitch. You better watch it." The girl shoved Julie's shoulder, then pushed through us into the changing room.

The other girls ignored us, looking away.

A part of me was relieved that the girl hadn't meant me, but Julie's lip curled, her eyebrows knit, and her eyes begin to water and flood. Pools formed along her rims, then splashed over and down, forming streams down her cheeks.

"I have to go," I muttered, walking away as quickly as I could. By the time I had changed, Julie was gone. The skirt she'd been wearing was on the floor, forgotten and abandoned.

The next Saturday, Julie's mother sat on the bench outside, observing us intently as we moved through class.

I'd hoped to avoid Julie in the changing room, but she never came in. As the shuffle into the studio began, I saw her standing by the entrance. The woman beside her had a Louis Vuitton purse hanging from her forearm and large gold earrings peeking out from beneath her bobbed hair. A sweater draped over her shoulders, the sleeves knotted in front of her collarbones, which protruded from beneath her white polo shirt. She was tan and pretty. Looking at her, I imagined what Julie would look like when she grew older.

Like the other girls, I took the same place on the barre that I had the week before. Julie came over and stood next to me.

"Hi Anna," she said.

I looked away. "Hi." I bent down to fuss with the elastic on my shoes, poking my finger inside the arches.

The girl who'd called Julie a bitch stood a few girls behind us, glaring at me whenever she caught me looking at her reflection. Julie's movements were measured and careful. I did my best to imitate her, but she wasn't as graceful as she'd been before. Still, Mrs. Sato didn't correct a thing, but neither did she praise her as she did before.

After soon as class was over, I rushed out without saying goodbye. Instead of changing out of my dance clothes, I threw on my jeans and hurriedly pulled my T-shirt over my head. Because I'd worn slippers to class that day, I wedged the rubber between my toes, stretching the fabric of my tights.

I dashed out the changing room to see Julie and her mom talking with Mrs. Sato. I sped past them, heading for the driveway, hoping my mother's car would be there.

"Anna!"

I ignored Julie's voice and continued walking.

"Anna, wait!"

I couldn't pretend I hadn't heard. Julie looked so fragile, glancing around and over her shoulder. She craned her neck. Her mother in eyesight, she turned back to me.

"I'm not going to be in class anymore."

I couldn't imagine that Julie was going to quit.

"How come?"

She looked down and pointed her toe.

"Mrs. Sato is moving me to Beginner 2. My mom talked to her and asked her if I could. I guess they think it's okay. I was in Intermediate with my other teacher."

"Oh." I looked over at Mrs. Sato's driveway.

"So I guess I'm not going to see you in class anymore. Well, I mean, I'll see you in between."

"Yeah, I'll see you in between." I avoided her eyes.

Julie was staring at me sadly. I began to get angry. We weren't really friends anyway, and I hated that she was acting like I'd done something wrong.

"Anna," she said.

"What?" I was relieved to see that my mother had just pulled in. "My mom's here."

"Nothing." Julie chewed on her lower lip. "Just, when you do your arm positions, relax your hands more. Don't make them into a cup."

"Okay." I ran to my mother's car without looking back. "Whatever," I mumbled.

I hopped into the car, relieved.

"Is that your friend?" my mother asked.

Julie stood on the grass. When she saw me look in her direction, she waved.

"No. She's just some girl from class. She's quitting."

My mother tilted her head, watching Julie as she walked towards the studio. She walked a lot like Mrs. Sato.

"That's too bad. She looks like she would make a good dancer."

We pulled out of the driveway, and I saw Julie and her mother standing together. I wanted her to fall, to break her leg.

"She's not that good. That's why she's quitting."

I pressed the button to roll up the window. Soon, the sound of air conditioning drowned out the sounds, the things outside us visible, but unheard.

When I got home, I stood in front of the mirror. I hated the body looking back at me. I wished my mother had married a different man, one who was tall and graceful like she was, one who could make me pretty and thin. One who didn't die when I was a baby. I wished my father would go away.

Over the months, my body absorbed the tap of Mrs. Sato's yardstick keeping time to the music until it beat inside of me like a second pulse. Where my limbs once moved in the general direction of each position, I began to detect limits—where to stop the pivot of my thighbone, how much to rotate my arms in their sockets, at what tension to pull my shoulder blades closer. I was discovering the shape of a ballerina, filling its form. Over the next two years, my hips opened, and my feet slowly turned out like the hands of a clock, a badge all the girls wore with pride. My movements became liquid, and there was a tiny bounce in each of my steps—the smallest lift, as if each one were the practice of flying and a sure sign that I was closer to going en pointe.

When I thought of Julie, it wasn't her dancing that I recalled. It was the way she had sunk so quickly after floating so high. She was still one level ahead of me, and it didn't take long for our bond to dissolve. The strained hellos and eye contact soon gave way, and we simply became molecules in the stream of bodies flowing in the passage between the changing room and the studio. The girl who had bullied her had left after the first level, and without her and Julie, I could dance unfettered. Alone, I drew Mrs. Sato's instruction in, her voice the impulse directing my body, working its way into micro-movements that pivoted me across the floor.

There were no other ballet dancers in my grade, and like everyone around me, what I did outside of school came to define me. It was easy to fall into the role. I let the label drape itself over me. Soon, everyone could only see the part I played. Even when I wasn't in class, I began wearing my hair pulled back in a bun that I wound neatly and pinned tight to my head, its taut grip holding me together.

My mother watched my progress with a sacred pride, as if it were she who was dancing on stage. She faithfully came to every recital, always bringing me a single rose. She beamed at me in a way I had never before seen, and I basked in her admiration as if it were a drug. I sometimes sensed she wanted to talk, to tell me what I might do to improve my technique, but she withheld her comments as much as I retreated from them. And though I was still no match for her when she was my age, I felt less distant from her beauty, delighting in what I perceived as the increasing twinning of our movements.

Once, when I was in my room, slipping on a loose white chemise that was our costume for an upcoming recital, she stood in the doorway and exclaimed, "Anna-sshi, you look just like a real dancer!" As she smiled at me, I wondered if she could perhaps see herself. I wondered if, for my mother, I had become like her, if I had transcended the physicality of my father. I was still short and my body broad, so far from Tracy Kuroda, whose collarbones floated up from the neckline of her leotard. No one knew if she really starved herself, but with gravity pulling far less on her than it did on the rest of the class, she sailed and twirled with an enviable ease. But neither was I like Jennifer Lee, so thick and muscular that Mrs. Sato never placed her in the front. I hovered comfortably in the middle, safely between the spotlight and invisibility.

My mother and I maintained the ritual of our monthly Sunday trips to the beach, though we went later in the day, nearly right before sunset, because I didn't want my skin to darken. I had long ago abandoned my obligation to step into the water, and would sit instead with her on the sand, tiny strands of hair loosening and brushing my face.

Once, we sat on a blanket in the last moments of daylight. Knife in hand, my mother spun an apple slowly, the long curl of skin that dangled so transparent that I could see the light coming through it in parts.

I had always loved the way she cut fruit, the slices symmetric and without divots or nicks, so clean that I could reassemble the pieces into naked apples or pears, whatever she'd chosen.

"In Korea, people judge you by how well you cut fruit. The better you do it, the better wife you will be," she said.

I looked at her in disbelief, making a face. "If I ever go to Korea, I'm going to cut crooked. I don't want to marry someone who cares if I can cut his food."

She laughed. I thought it meant I'd amused her.

"So Dad cared how well you cut fruit?" Hugging my knees to my chest, I traced a semicircle in the sand with my big toe.

She continued her work, the soft scraping sound of her knife like the hush of the waves.

"Well, your dad wasn't really Korean." She bit her lower lip, something she did whenever she was concentrating. "I mean, your dad wasn't raised in Korea. Your dad is from here. So it's different.

He didn't care about that. But your grandma did."

My grandmother had died before I was born, shortly after my mom and dad married, leaving the property she had accumulated to her only child. When I looked at her picture, she seemed like a stranger. I couldn't fathom that we were actually related.

"Oh, she gave me a hard time!" my mother laughed.

"How?" I tried to imagine the face in the pictures yelling at my mother.

"If you marry a Korean, then you'll see."

I'd never been to Korea, knew almost nothing about it. It was unremarkable to me on the map, no different from China or Japan or the Philippines. I knew it was where my mother had grown up, but her existence before me was hazy and irrelevant.

"I'm never going to marry a Korean. In fact, I'm never going to get married."

The skin fell to the plate she had brought, a ghost of what it used to be.

My mother held the apple in her hand. "You don't want to get married?"

I glanced out to the water.

"I don't think I need to. You're okay without Dad here."

She knit her brows and looked at me. "Anna-sshi, I miss your dad every day."

"But it's been so long. He's not even here," I said. "It's almost like he never existed." I kicked some sand, ruining the perfect semicircle I had drawn before.

My mother said nothing. She put the apple down onto the plastic cutting board and carefully quartered it, then into eighths. As she removed the core, cutting an even vee into each slice, she said, "Every time I look at you, I see your father."

I stayed quiet, not knowing what to say.

"Why do you think we live how we do? Why do you think you have a nice house, nice clothes, can take ballet lessons? Why do you think we're here and not in Korea living with my mother in Seoul?"

I looked down at my toes.

"Why do you think you can sit here on the beach and look at the water in this place that everyone calls paradise? You think all this just happened?" Although she spoke softly, her voice was sharp.

"We have all this because your dad died, Anna. We have all this because your halmeoni left it to him, and then because he left it to me. Your dad is here. Your dad is here taking care of you every single day." The knife hit the cutting board with a clack as she put it down. The slices rolled on their rounded backs.

She took out two small forks she had brought from home, spearing a slice of apple with each one. She held mine out to me. "Here," she said. Her voice was still harsh, angry.

I reached for the fork, the cool handle smooth between my fingers, then took small bites, forcing myself to swallow.

The sight of the sand beneath my feet blurred and softened, its texture the same as when I looked at the sea.

I couldn't remember him even with pictures. I was too young when he was killed in the crash out near Wai'anae, when another car crossed over the line and hit him head-on. I didn't know what he was doing or why he was there. I knew I had been at the funeral, but I couldn't conjure any memory of it or of anything else, of his voice or his face, or the way he held me after I was born. I knew his touch was locked somewhere in my cells, but I couldn't get it to rise to the surface. Instead, I thought of him as never existing except when I looked too carefully at myself in the mirror.

My mother kept his photos in an old black album, the kind with stickers to hold down the corners. It sat on the bottom shelf of our bookcase, below her copies of the books she loved by James Joyce, Thomas Hardy, and Nathaniel Hawthorne.

Tugging the album out of its slot, I made note of its exact placement among the ones I was more familiar with—my baby album, the pictures from elementary school and junior high. My mother wasn't home, but I took my father's album into my room, making sure to close the door behind me.

I'd seen those pictures several times before, when my mother would be telling me a story about him, stopping to pull the album out and show me the moment she recalled, or on the days I felt sheer curiosity, wanting to see his face, too remote to affect me.

But this time, I felt as if I were eavesdropping on a secret, the information seductive but classified.

The first photo was of their wedding in Korea. Next to my mother, my father looked big, but she told me he wasn't very tall, which her family didn't like. As with tradition, neither of them smiled, but if I looked close enough, I could see how their eyes were transparent mirrors that, just beneath the surface, revealed their joy.

I flipped past the wedding picture and several other pages until I got to the photo I was looking for. When I saw it, I froze for just a moment, the shock of it something I didn't expect. In it, my father stood at the Pali Lookout, the wind pushing his hair against the back of his head. His left hand held closed the collar of his polo shirt, his wedding band visible, and his eyes squinted just a little against the sun as he maintained a smile for the shot. Behind him, the Ko'olau mountains and bright blue water stretched into the distance, beautiful but hiding the fatal drop below.

I could see how I was my father's daughter, how sometimes I even stood as he did, my hip pushed out to the right with my shoulders hunched slightly forward. I could see how our faces were even shaped the same, round with smooth foreheads curved out like a bowl. It didn't take much to see how strong the resemblance ran, but it wasn't for that that I wanted this picture. It was for the teenaged girl that stood beside him, leaning against the wall with her arms crossed in front of her chest. Her hair was long and straight, and she looked maybe Chinese, her face, too, turned toward the camera. But her eyes revealed an angry sadness, and each time I looked at this picture, it was her I saw. I often wondered who was just out of the frame, and if she felt unloved or if she was alone.

That had been almost fifteen years ago. By now, she might have been maybe thirty years old. I wondered if she had married or moved away, or if maybe, if her life just hadn't gone right, she had come back to the Pali to leap from the cliff.

I couldn't help feeling that no one saw her, my father's and mother's gaze locked on each other. I couldn't help feeling she was outside of their bond, watching their closeness, but invisible.

I was so absorbed in staring at the picture that I didn't hear my mother's car pull up outside. Her keys unlocked the front door and she called out to me. I slammed the album shut, wondering whether or not to shove it under my bed.

I walked out to the kitchen, where she was putting away groceries from her Saturday shopping. In her hands, she held fresh fish wrapped in pink butcher paper that she'd gotten from Chinatown.

"Do you need help?" My heart pounded as I tried to appear calm.

"You can put away the vegetables for me," she said, sliding the fish into the refrigerator and stepping back to dig green onions, cabbage, turnips, and bean sprouts out of the grocery bags, handing them to me one by one. "Did you finish studying?"

"Yeah. Sort of. I still have to write my paper for English."

When she left the kitchen to change her clothes, I ran back to my room, then placed the photo album exactly where it had been.

That night, I took a pair of scissors and gave myself bangs. I chopped quickly and angrily, feeling a strange satisfaction when the dark strands fell in the sink. They were jagged and short, hovering above my brows. When my mother saw them, she gasped and sighed, then took me by the wrist into the bathroom, painstakingly working until the lines were clean, a sharp dark edge cutting across my forehead.

"Bangs, huh?"

Karen tugged on her legwarmers as I walked into the studio.

I shrugged my shoulders. "No big deal." I settled in next to her, placing my heel on the barre, leaning forward to stretch my legs.

"You look punk. Why'd you cut them so short?" She rested on her elbows, leaning heavily against the barre, something that made Mrs. Sato yell if she saw us doing it.

"Got sick of having them in my face. Why, you want me to cut yours, too?" I reached for her head as she ducked away.

Mrs. Sato made her entrance, her yardstick at her side. We all fell into line, as was the drill. We ran through our pliés, our elevés, then moved to our positions on the floor. Because Karen was little and didn't break a hundred pounds, she danced in front with Tracy Kuroda. I stood behind Tracy, in the middle of the second row.

Tracy's shoulder blades jutted out, and I couldn't help watching the knobs of her spine poke through her leotard whenever she bowed forward. They were like a path of rocks running down her back.

When I had watched one too many times, Mrs. Sato's yardstick whacked the floor in front of me.

"You girls need to remember the moves for yourself. You can't always rely on the others around you. Eyes up." She glanced at me admonishingly.

I fixed my gaze straight ahead, looking at a spot in the mirror over Tracy's left shoulder. I caught Karen looking at me and rolling her eyes.

As we moved to the music of *Swan Lake*, I wondered if my shoulder blades too slid on my back like wings. I knew they were there, buried under flesh and muscle. I knew they were there, just like Tracy's. The difference was that she had managed to eliminate what was in between, to allow the smallest distance between surface and bone.

After class, Karen walked with me out to the driveway.

"Is it me or is Tracy getting thinner?"

"That girl needs a pizza," said Karen, fishing around in her bag. Her hand emerged clutching a pack of Skittles.

"Don't let Mrs. Sato see that." Most of the time when I saw Karen, she was munching on chips or chocolate, not almonds or dried cranberries like some of the other girls.

Karen tossed a handful of the Skittles into her mouth. "I metabolize fast, so it's none of her business."

"I'm serious. Doesn't it seem like Tracy lost weight?"

"Duh, we're in ballet. Institutionalized eating disorders? I'd be more shocked if she wasn't puking." Karen popped more Skittles. "Our school's having a dance tonight. With *boys.*"

A silver Lexus pulled up to the driveway. Karen's mom waved at me. I waved back as Karen headed for the car. As she walked away from me, she whispered mockingly, "Tell Tracy to eat something—it gives you boobs."

I rolled my eyes and waved goodbye as she got into the passenger seat.

It was then that I noticed Tracy stood all the way at the edge of the grass where it met the pavement of the driveway. She never seemed to talk to anyone, just came for class then left right after. For all of her grandeur and grace in class, she seemed to shrink outside of the studio.

The bones of her chest seemed more pronounced in sunlight. If I didn't look carefully, I could almost mistake her for a much older woman.

She caught me watching her and quickly looked down at the ground. Just then, my mother's car pulled in.

I got in, but kept my eyes on Tracy's reflection in the side-mirror.

"Anna-sshi, how was class?" My mother handed me a can of juice, knowing how thirsty I got.

"It was good. Everyone liked my bangs."

That night, as I lay in bed, I couldn't stop picturing Tracy's bones. It seemed each day the girls at school accumulated flesh, forming breasts and hips and curves at their waists. Tracy was working by subtraction. I wondered how soon it'd be until she was invisible. I wondered if she would eventually turn to air, indistinguishable from the space in which she sailed.

The rain fell so hard that the drops slammed against the side of the house. The wind rattled the screens and moved the drumming sounds left and right, sometimes harder, sometimes softer. I lay on my bed, my legs propped against the wall, listening to the creaking wood, the storm orchestrated by the gusts.

It had been pouring for three days, dissolving the ground into a watery mass. Boys like Matt Shima and Carter Chang wore their gym clothes after getting detention for starting mud fights. The girls came to school in mini-skirts and slippers, cleaning their feet and legs with the hose by the cafeteria, leaving pools of footprints in their wake. Everything in the rooms felt damp, the tops of the desks sticky, notebook pages wilted and soft. Moist air weighted the tips of our hair and saturated our clothing. From class to class, we trudged through halls filled with humid sighs and languid exhales.

At home, wetness seeped into everything. I didn't feel like starting my homework. Instead, I pushed my back into the clammy bedspread beneath me, pressing my fingers into my belly, gravity hollowing it into a bowl.

My mother knocked on my open door and leaned in.

"Anna-sshi, the soup is on the stove. Start the rice about half an hour before you want to eat, okay?"

I twisted my neck to look back at her.

"Okay." She was wearing her charcoal grey blouse and black pencil skirt, her double-strand pearls, and her pearl and diamond earrings. When she dressed up, she looked like someone who came from someplace else, like someone who came from a more glamorous time.

"Did you start your studying?"

"I finished everything at school today."

She smiled and reached up to check one of her earrings.

"You're such a good girl."

I could smell her perfume from where she stood at the door. It drifted in like a tendril.

"I won't be long," she said. "Mrs. Lee gets very tired these days and likes to sleep early." Mrs. Lee was new to our church and had just moved from San Bernardino to Hawai'i. She and my mother had become friends after she found out they had both lost their husbands.

"Okay."

"Eat plenty, okay?"

I heard her footsteps retreat down the hall and into the kitchen, then the knock of her high heels against the floor as she put them on. The door shut behind her, followed by the click and shunt of the lock and deadbolt. Her car engine pitched itself awake, growing softer as she disappeared.

I could still smell her perfume in the air.

Inside the house was still and heavy. The silence pressed down on me until my thoughts crawled out of their hiding places and came out into the open.

The first time I had seen Jason, he slunk down the hall dragging his feet, the hem of his too-long jeans worn and frayed. Everyone knew his story, how he was kicked out of private school for drinking then showed up mid-semester to finish his junior year. He was a year ahead of me and kept mostly to himself, though I sometimes saw him with Matt and Carter. He didn't seem like the type who would start a fight, but he didn't seem like the kind who would avoid one, either. For the most part, people left him alone. But there was something about the way he was so quiet and his hair hung in his eyes that made me stare. The first time he caught me, he was out in the courtyard, sitting on one of the benches while Matt and Carter were copying homework from each other. His eyes stayed on mine, and I glanced away. The next time he caught me, I was shocked by the small tug of his lips into a half-smirk. His gaze pulled me in, swallowing mine.

Over the next few days, I saw him at lunchtime, in between classes, after school. It seemed like every time, he'd catch me watching him. I was embarrassed that he'd spotted me, that I wasn't anonymous like the rest of the girls. Still, every moment outside of class felt charged. I found myself looking for him, wanting to see him, but I was afraid to, mostly because I wasn't sure what would come next.

One morning when I got to school, he was leaning against the wall outside his homeroom. He had his books under his arm and kept his gaze forward, unaffected by the chatter and bustle of the bodies before him. I had to walk past him to get to my locker. My heart was pounding and I felt myself flush. I hoped that maybe he wouldn't see me in the crowd.

I tried to keep my eyes down and pretend I didn't see him in my periphery, but at the last moment, something made me turn my head. When I did, the same half-smile was on his lips. I broke into a trot and hurried toward my locker.

The rest of the day I tried desperately to avoid him. I was almost tardy for all my classes, ate my lunch in the classroom instead of the cafeteria. Where I thought he'd be, I tried to avoid. I couldn't imagine that he'd take an interest in me. There was nothing in my body that invited boys. But something had been established, and now, the consequences hung heavy around me, like thoughts I had before falling asleep. I had somehow invited him in, and I didn't know how to go backwards without having to push.

That was the day the rain started falling. All afternoon, the air had been dense with the coming storm. A few minutes before school let out, it slapped down on the roof like applause. I was grateful my mom picked me up every day, not like the kids who caught the bus home. As soon as the bell rang, I dashed out and ran to my locker to grab the rest of my books.

I didn't see him in the halls, and I knew my mother would be coming soon. As I stood at the top of the stairs leading out of the building, water dripping down from the clogged gutters and bodies pushing past me to run into the street toward buses and cars and whatever shelter there was, I felt someone standing behind me.

"I can give you a ride."

I hadn't heard him speak before, and his voice, even though it was more or less ordinary, surprised me. His hair was wet and hanging in his face. I could smell cigarette smoke on his clothing.

My body tensed. "That's okay. My mom is coming." I turned away, afraid that he would notice I was shaking, afraid that someone would see us together, afraid that someone might point and whisper, exposing my longing for others to see.

"You dance?" His voice was soft.

I didn't want to look him in the eye. "Yeah." I kept my focus on the street. "But I'm not great or anything." My mother's car pulled up. Most of me wanted to run, but part of me sank, wishing desperately that she had come just a few minutes later.

"Um, I have to go."

I started down the stairs, but he tugged my arm. I flinched from the unexpected contact. I wondered if I looked like I thought he would hurt me.

For a moment, I wasn't sure if he was going to say something or if he was going to hold me there, but he let go of me and smiled.

I glanced at him awkwardly then ran into the rain, down the long walkway and into the car.

My mother squinted through the timing of the windshield wipers in Jason's direction. "Who is that, Anna-sshi?"

I threw my things in the backseat. "Just a guy."

She glanced at me. "How come you didn't use your umbrella?"

"It's in my backpack."

She paused, as if she wanted to say something more, but she put the car in gear and began driving instead. We used to talk on the drive home, but lately, the radio had begun to fill the space between us. I wanted to be alone with my thoughts, so I slid into the camouflage of pop music and public radio.

I pulled down the visor to see if I could make out Jason's

shape in the reflection of the mirror. I saw the stairs, but he had gone. I wondered how long he'd had his license and what would've happened if I even had a chance to say yes.

I didn't tell my mother about Jason. Instead, I spent the rest of the evening quietly pretending it was a night like any other. After dinner, I helped her wash the dishes and clean the kitchen, our usual routine except on nights before big tests.

She kept glass containers in neat stacks on the shelf. She didn't like plastic because she said it smelled. I carefully pulled a smaller one out, making sure not to disturb the delicate stack and send it crashing to the ground. My mother handed me the bowl of kong namul and a clean pair of chopsticks so that I could put the leftovers away. The thin, stringy roots of each bean sprout had been pinched off because she thought it was cleaner that way. I remember when I was little, noticing that the kong namul at the restaurants looked wild, messy, sometimes catching in my teeth.

A part of me wanted to ask her about Jason, but I didn't know what to ask. I didn't know if she could understand—she had been so beautiful that I couldn't imagine her being flustered by a boy. I knew, though, that she had to have liked boys before she met my father, had to remember what it was like. I opened my mouth to speak, but the sight of her back as she cleared the table stopped me. I returned instead to lifting clumps of sprouts soaked in shoyu and sesame oil, placing them carefully into the container.

Once everything had been put away, I walked over to the sink and picked up the netted cloth, dunking it in hot water and sudsing the dishes. It was her turn to rinse. We stood side by side, our movements so timed that we no longer had to think of them.

I hadn't been able to stop thinking of Jason, that night or even the next morning when I awoke. After I washed up and ate breakfast, I ruffled through my closet over and over again. It was still raining and I didn't want to wear jeans. I hated the way the water soaked into the hems, weighting my legs, but my skirts were in the laundry, so I couldn't wear them, either. I finally chose a dress, my short blue one, throwing on a hoodie to cover my shoulders.

The car radio was tuned the classical station. The piano concerto softened the atmosphere inside the car, making me feel warm and dry. The only thing I could picture was Jason, his long hair, his shirtsleeves rolled up to his forearms, the way he walked. Again, I thought of asking my mother about Jason, but I didn't know how to start. I searched for the words that would open my chest so my heart could flood out instead of churning inside.

"Use your umbrella this time," my mother said as we pulled up. I fished it out of my backpack and opened the door just wide enough for me to poke it out and open it, where it formed a wide shelter. I said goodbye and let myself out. This time, I didn't run. Instead, I tilted the umbrella against the direction of the rain and let the drops of water pelt the nylon and bounce away.

Part of me was disappointed that Jason wasn't there at the top of the stairs. In fact, he wasn't even in school.

But the next morning, he was. When I saw him, I folded my umbrella, shaking it over and over again to dry it off until he took it from my hands and I followed him inside. We walked wordlessly, letting looks of surprise rain upon us all day.

The bell rang to release us. He'd taken me outside by the side of the gym, where the stairs above us kept us dry. I couldn't tell if my heart was pounding because of him or because I was afraid we'd get in trouble. Jason told me nobody ever went there, that that's where he went when he wanted to smoke. I could hear the sound of voices interspersed with rain. Everyone was too busy getting home, running into cars and bus shelters, hovering in the halls to care about us. I was terrified of being there and I'd never been alone with a boy. I couldn't stop shaking and felt stupid and ugly, but Jason held my hand and pulled me close where I shook so hard that I thought he did, too. For what seemed like a long time, we stood that way, his one hand holding mine, the other slipped around my waist. He leaned his forehead against mine, his face so close that I could feel his breath. I started to panic.

"I can't stay. My mom is coming. She comes—she comes right after school. I have to go." I stepped back and tried to drop his hand, but he drew me closer again where his body was warm. Just like that day he stood behind me, I wanted to run, but I wanted more to stay.

Jason drew back his head to look at me.

"You're really pretty."

I was too confused to say he was wrong. And then he reached around to touch my hair. I felt his fingers tangled in my bun and before I knew it, my hair had fallen loose down my back.

I saw her car in the distance as I ran towards it, so much mud splashing that I felt it spatter the backs of my thighs. She couldn't have been waiting for more than five minutes, but I ran as if she'd been there for hours. I hurriedly twisted my wet hair up, tucking the loose ends in as best as I could. The pins had dropped to the ground and I hadn't stopped to pick them up.

I grasped the handle and threw the door open. "I'm sorry, Mom! I'm so sorry!"

"Anna-sshi, what happened? Where were you?"

I started to say that I had come from P.E., that I lost track of time and had been in the showers, but instead, I began to cry, until I was sobbing so hard I could no longer speak.

When we got home, I told her I was worried that I was flunking math, that the teacher was so hard that he never gave A's. She kissed me and made me some ginger tea and asked if I wanted her to stay home with me. She said Mrs. Lee would understand.

I told her to go and that I wanted to rest. I hadn't been able to tell her that Jason even existed, and talking about him now seemed more than impossible.

I could still feel his lips on my neck, his hands under my clothes, the way he buried his face in my hair. I was too scared to do anything but stand completely still. He kissed me again and again, my head pressed against the wall behind me. I stayed pinned beneath him, terrified that someone would see us. And when he pulled away, I grabbed my bag and started to run, gasping for air as I crossed the field.

Lying on my bed, I let myself linger on what I'd been too scared to feel, bringing Jason back until he was there. The rain pounded the roof in crescendo and diminuendo. My hands traveled over and down my body, slipping quietly between my thighs, where I imagined Jason until my fingers emerged wet, just like the storm.

Thicker Than Water

To move in water is to move without limit;
unbound by gravity, you glide and turn
with the ease of creatures
whose moment-to-moment existence escapes
the tiled floors, well-worn carpets,
the waxed surfaces that now pave your days.
It is no wonder in sleep you gasp for air.
At the end of summer, there is no breeze—
trapped in thick, humid air,
your mother enumerates the things she loves.
It was in her belly you first learned to float,
she, your tether to an earth-bound world.
Now she prepares to take her leave,
her body quieted by the cancer of women who give too much,
and in these moments you crave with untold longing
the watery innocence of your formation,
mourn your body's denial of liquid grace
as cars collide, trains derail,
streets and sidewalks lock us into lines and crossings.
If only we could move like particles of waves,
all directions open for the price of a breath,
fluid density all but erasing the impact of blows.
Each time your steps lift from sand to sea,
immersion recalls your very creation,
the rightness of suspension when you shared one body,
the sea around you a tangible promise
that when the time comes for you to emerge
she will cherish your breaths,
sweep your cobwebs,
drink your sighs,
and cushion your sleep,

that no matter how far you stray from her touch,
you will feel the echo of her tether,
less constraint than her reminder of how you are never alone,
that even in the spacious depths of the universe,
in that windless place that carries no sound,
gossamer threads spin down to cradle you softly
while stars dance to her lullaby.

가막

어둠

백매

수상

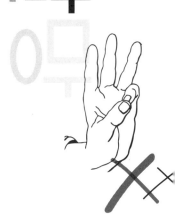

Natural Disasters

Thousands of miles apart
and in different time zones,
you and I laugh about
the fundamental rightness of banjos
and the perfect logic
in becoming rock stars
should we fail to find jobs.
Though you tell me you've changed,
that the displacement of home
has made you ugly,
all I see is the continuing beauty of you,
and why, when we shop for shoes,
you will put one on your head
to signal your need for help.
No one laughs at our jokes.
Together, we create disturbance:
short French men
are cast out of pubs;
grumpy tattoo artists
explain that
there is no such thing
as a two-for-one sale;
newly-minted bartenders
dance vigorously to nonexistent music
to disguise their discomfort.
All this from trying to get a drink
in a town called L.A.
Thousands of miles apart,
and in different time zones,
we are still natural disasters.
Together, we marvel

at the destruction that trails us.
No one questions a hurricane.
Named, watched, feared,
it simply does what it must.
Damage is incidental,
and almost always by accident.

Everyday Practice

The water rolling off his back should've made him feel clean, but like a ritual whose meaning had been lost over time and countless repetitions, showering was perfunctory, just something he did each morning because he had always done so. In exactly eight minutes, he would be done. He didn't even need to look at his watch. In fact, he didn't even need to wear it in the shower, but since it was waterproof, he felt obligated to use it to its full capacity. Everything about his morning was a perfectly timed routine, so when he stepped out of the tub and into the puddle of urine the cat had left as punishment for yet another one of his unwitting crimes, he simply reached for the paper towels and vinegar-water solution he kept nearby for just such occasions, cleaned up the mess, and went on with his business. He paused to swear at the calico that glared at him with disgust, but mostly because he felt it was appropriate to do so. The cat took in his half-hearted litany of curse words with ears flattened, and stared, unblinking.

The cat had been a present from an ex-girlfriend. Like the ex, the cat was comforted at first by his gentle and quiet nature until she discovered that his equanimity was really a lack of initiative. The girlfriend left, but the cat stayed; he hadn't bothered to find her another home, so he purchased the same food, treats, and kitty litter they had always purchased before when they were a "family," as his ex liked to say. Now he was a single father subject to the humiliation of cohabitating with a dependent who saw him as an annoyance whose value was arguably little more than that of a vending machine. It was a good thing he didn't care.

He had been alone, so to speak, for a little less than three months now, a passage of time he'd begun to dread because his friends, not to mention his family, believed that eight weeks was sufficient to mourn a five-month relationship and had consequently exhibited increasingly aggressive attempts to get him "out there."

The first attempt, courtesy of his sister's coworker, was a transplant from Manhattan who'd moved to Hawai'i to explore real estate. She talked incessantly about her difficulties with dating men who were threatened by her ambition and recited names of ex-lovers who, rather than admiring her go-getting attitude and business savvy, competed mercilessly with her until she'd been forced to admit that it wasn't working. She'd hoped Hawai'i would be different. She believed that a state once ruled by a queen had to breed men accustomed to a strong woman. She asked him when they would meet next, a question he answered with a shrug which was, judging by her reaction, an entirely unacceptable response.

In the ensuing discussions, a network of friends, family, and coworkers decided that while he did need a woman who could take charge and hold the reins, that perhaps he should be paired with someone who, while still willing to lead the carriage, wouldn't drive the horses to their death. They believed that transplants were the way to go, in case his reputation as a sweet but unambitious partner preceded him on this small island. However, New York being the opposite geographically and, in the opinions of some, culturally from Hawai'i, they settled on something West Coast—but not Los Angeles.

That's how Debbie came into the picture. His aunt had been shopping for a barbeque grill at Costco when an attractive young woman strolled by, her cart filled with forty-eight rolls of toilet paper, a wheel of cheddar cheese, a case of Perrier, and three bottles of wine. A single gal if she'd ever spotted one. His aunt began conversation with her by asking if she cooked very much, then noticed that the woman, who'd looked as if she could've been local (though one of those girls who graduated from Punahou or Mid-Pac), had an accent, "da kine haole kine," as his aunt later explained. Debbie was from Seattle and had come to Hawai'i because her father's family had been from the islands. She worked as a travel agent on Kapi'olani, and no, she didn't have a boyfriend, but yes, she was looking. By the time his aunt had gotten done with

Debbie, she had arranged for her to come to a family barbeque the following Sunday.

His aunt had paid him the courtesy of notifying him in advance of the set-up, but exhibited frustration at his reluctance to get a haircut. She told him that Debbie was "fancy," that he couldn't expect to win her over sitting in his shorts and T-shirt with a beer in his hand. He'd wanted to tell her that he wasn't planning to "win her over," but kept his mouth shut and opted for her berating him instead. Debbie was pretty and kind, smart and funny, but the more he saw that she was indeed a "nice girl," the more he felt he would just disappoint her in the end. He spent the rest of the evening on a fold-out chair in the garage, sandwiched safely between his two 'ukulele-toting cousins, who were attempting to harmonize on Tracy Chapman's "Baby Can I Hold You Tonight" and failing miserably.

His apparent disinterest in finding a new girlfriend prompted numerous calls from his mother. She worried that he was getting too old to meet someone and appealed to his need for personal happiness, but every once in a while, when she felt particularly distressed by his apathy, pulled out the "your father and I want to see our only son's children before we die" card, to which he unfailingly retorted that she was only fifty-six and that at twenty-nine, he wasn't no "old fut."

He didn't understand what the fuss was about. Yes, he missed Carla, but that wasn't the reason he didn't want another girlfriend. He knew she needed more, deserved a boyfriend who would make plans, surprise her with romantic evenings and home-cooked meals, spend hours talking with her about her dreams and problems and cares. When Carla left, he felt somewhat relieved that he would no longer let her down, something he'd begun to feel during the second week of their relationship, but not enough to actually break up with her.

What no one understood was that he was tired of having a girlfriend just because he was supposed to. Just as he was tired of wearing aloha shirts to work because he was supposed to. And, because he was supposed to, driving a Toyota truck or any number of other things that constituted his existence. His life had become an endless list of *supposed to's*; it shook him the day he realized that love fell on that list, too. He wanted love to be more than an everyday practice; he wanted to hear Aerosmith's "I Don't Want to Miss a Thing" in his head when he held a girl, or imagine kissing her in a soft-focus slow-motion music video. He wanted to feel like exchanging secret smiles with her while they were at some office function, writing her poems on notes left on the bathroom mirror, making love to her with something other than slow jams playing in the background.

When he thought all the way back to Marcy Takamine, his first girlfriend in the tenth grade, he realized he'd never really been in love. He'd always wanted to be, but this last episode with Carla—whom he thought he might very well marry if she could put up with him indefinitely—made him realize the whole thing seemed hopeless.

What confused him even more was that he *liked* his aloha shirts and truck. And he *liked* having a girlfriend. He never understood how someone would want to wander around from place to place without a steady job, or how someone could be happy just riding a bicycle for transportation. He wasn't the kind of person who liked to travel unless there were nice hotels, or watch movies that weren't in English, or buy strange musical instruments just to see what sounds they would make, like his cousin. That was the opposite of who he was. His life wasn't bad, but he hated feeling as if he were just going through the motions. He didn't know where the meaning had gone. Or how to get it back.

His watch read 7:13 a.m. He'd already showered, shaved, eaten breakfast, and dressed. He slipped his keys off the hook near the door and reached for his shoes. The location of the odor registered a moment too late. Only after he slid his foot halfway into his shoe did he feel the warm, hard lumps under his right foot. He glanced over at the cat crouching a few feet away, her tail swishing back and forth in vengeful delight. He groaned. The cat had subjected him to her urinating on his bed, clawing his lauhala mat to pieces, and vomiting in various locations in his kitchen, but this was new. It was 7:14. He always left at 7:15.

He was going to be late.

Stupid cat, he thought. Why hadn't Carla just taken it with her? She kept insisting it was a gift, that she couldn't take something she knew he needed. He'd told her he didn't need a cat, but she had walked out the door with a Macy's shopping bag full of clothes, toiletries, CDs, and kitchen items, and he hadn't heard from her since. He'd never wanted a cat in the first place, but thought it'd be rude to object. The cat did whatever she wanted, bit him when she didn't feel like being petted, and seemed to take delight in the fact that her stare unnerved him. In fact, she was doing it now. She locked her eyes on his perplexed expression, her unblinking gaze daring him to do something, anything, about her transgression. He stood gawking back at her, his right foot dangling in the air. The cat appeared amused.

It was 7:17.

"You're going to the pound!" he screamed, and whipped the soiled sock off his foot, stomped past her into the kitchen, and dumped it into the trash. He went back for his shoe, snatched it up angrily, and slammed it in after the sock, the crunchy thud of its impact giving him a small measure of satisfaction. He stalked back, his right foot naked, and pondered his next move. He had just the one pair of shoes he wore to work each day, the Kenneth Coles that Carla had encouraged him to buy on a Saturday afternoon when she'd dragged him to the outlet stores at Waikele. He glanced at the other shoes lined up by the door: a worn-down pair of Scott rubber slippers, his tired Adidas running shoes, and a dusty pair of hiking boots. He stood torn between putting on his running shoes and hightailing it to work, and fishing his proper shoe out of the trash, cleaning it up, and getting on with his day.

Because he was supposed to.

The words echoed in his head, slowly, like a mantra without the calming effect. He was always doing what he was supposed to do. Why couldn't he do what he *wasn't* supposed to do? So what if he didn't feel like getting a haircut for Debbie? Didn't he spend the rest of his life doing what he was supposed to do? What was one lousy haircut? A haircut he ended up getting in the end? Who was Debbie anyway? Just some girl his aunt picked out at Costco, like she was a bargain girlfriend or bulk-rate mate that he should feel like he got a deal on? Did his aunt even care if he liked her? The thing is, he had liked her. But the fact that he was *supposed* to like her made him *not* want to like her and he never thought of himself as the rebellious type and now he was and that made him even angrier. Carla used to tell him over and over again that she didn't think he loved her. He was supposed to love her, but he couldn't. But he tried, didn't he? *He* wasn't the one who left. *She* broke up with *him*! *She* left *him*! And so the thoughts continued, vaulting him into a two-minute tantrum in which he swore and cursed and tramped around loudly enough to prompt the cat to lift herself up and saunter out of the room. The sight of that along with his bare foot launched him into an even deeper frenzy. He whipped off his belt, shirt, and the rest of his clothing and hurled them in the direction she'd gone in. He gathered up the unsoiled Kenneth Cole, his slippers, Adidas, and hiking boots, and dunked them one-by-one into the trash with such fervent cursing that his neighbor Mrs. Chan banged on the adjoining wall.

It was 7:23.

He'd worked himself into a sweat.

The cat came back to investigate, nestling onto his rumpled shirt. She watched him as he panted in the middle of the room wearing nothing but his underwear, his hands clenching and unclenching and his breath coming out in small snorts.

He was fairly sure he looked ridiculous. And that he would begin to smell.

He shook his head, resigned, and with a sigh, trudged past the cat into the bathroom. He turned on the faucets: first hot, then cold, until both ran evenly. As he stepped into the shower, the water cascaded over his head and ran down his back. He stayed that way, trying to figure out when things had become so rote, so mechanical. What was the point of anything? He pressed his forehead against the tiles and closed his eyes. He wasn't sure how long he stood there, but he figured if he was going to be late, he was going to be late.

He reached for the soap, which was usually hard and dry and made a small smacking sound as it pulled free, and noticed that it was wet and squashy in his hand. Of course it would be. Although he was a two-shower-a-day guy—one in the morning and one before bed—he'd never taken two in a row before. He looked at his watch.

7:31.

The display looked strange in the shower, an odd combination completely out of context. It occurred to him that he had never seen those numbers before during his soaping stage. At 7:31, he was usually trying to merge into the right-hand lane of Kīna'u so he could turn down Ward. He'd be swearing vehemently under his breath when he couldn't cut over, only to smile and shaka enthusiastically at the very same driver when the recipient of his curses slowed down to let him in. Would the traffic be better or worse when he got to that merge now? If it were better, he might make up some of the time caused by the derailment of his schedule; but if it were worse, he'd be even more late. What would he say when he got there? That the cat took a dump in his Kenneth Cole? He was the guy who was never late, so everyone would be expecting something big. He wracked his brain, rapidly running the gamut from car trouble to food poisoning, but in the end, didn't feel right lying. Still, he couldn't tell them that several small lumps of cat feces put a ding in his perfect attendance record. He would tell them he was late because of...family problems. That was it. Carla had considered the cat family, so it wasn't really lying. And the cat did have a problem. After all, even though he never once felt the cat viewed him with anything less than insolent pity, she'd be lost without him. Who was she kidding? She needed him.

7:32.

He'd have been at the light now, waiting to turn on to Ward. Even though traffic would be too heavy for him or anyone else to make the right while the light was red, he'd mutter, "Go, faka, go!" anyway. The disparity between body memory and the reality of his actual locale began to eat at him. He didn't want to be late. He really preferred not to be. He *liked* being on time. He *liked* knowing that at 7:44, he could park on the fifth floor. He *liked* that once he walked into the office, Sherry would greet him with her just-a-hint-of-pidgin accent. He *liked* that his papers would be exactly where he left them the day before so he could pick up exactly where he left off. He even *liked* that he could expect Brad Koo to talk about how he was going to bang Sherry someday. What would happen if he walked in late? Would it all fall to pieces, launching him into reliving this feline criminal action over and over again?

No, he would not go down without a fight.

He rushed through the rest of his shower, and stepping out of his tub, instinctively reached for the paper towels and vinegar-water spray bottle before he realized the cat hadn't peed. He toweled off and ran to the closet for a fresh aloha shirt and slacks, running his fingers through his hair and whipping his belt up off the floor, furiously threading it through his belt loops. Jamming his feet into a new pair of socks, he sprinted to the door only to skid to a stop when he realized that all of his shoes were in the trash. And one of them still contained cat poop. His running shoes and hiking boots were both muddied and old, and cleaning them off would take just as much time, if not more, as cleaning the Kenneth Cole. He swept his gaze around the room desperately thinking.

Suddenly, his eyes locked on the hall closet. Racing over, he flung the door open and fished underneath the utility shelves until he found them. Strapping himself in, he wheeled back to the living room, marveling that he could still maneuver like a champ even though it'd been years since Linda Reyes made him go to Sports Authority to buy a matching pair of rollerblades so they could hold hands and skate at Ala Moana after work.

Whizzing past the cat, he noticed she was still on his aloha shirt. Her hind leg extended upward like a sundial gnomon as she cleaned her behind.

Slamming into the door, he picked up his keys, then and spun around.

Unaffected by the commotion, the cat dug in further under her tail.

"Nala!"

Nala lifted her head slightly, her leg still poised mid-air.

He hissed loudly at her, baring his teeth and scrunching his nose. Her foot drooped just a tad. After a brief pause, she stuck her head back between her legs and resumed her cleaning.

He sped down the hall.

7:38.

As he rolled into the elevator then out to his Toyota truck, something about the flashes of shiny black plastic on his feet caused him to chuckle. He increased his stride, picking up more and more speed as he rounded the corner to his parking lot, his breath a steady, forceful stream.

It was the right thing to do. After all, he was going to need to make up for lost time.

Cracks in the Wall

If there's one thing I've come to depend on, it's the stuff you don't have to think about when you first wake up. For instance, I know that if I slap my arm down toward the nightstand when I hear my alarm go off, it'll hit the general area of my snooze button, which will give me seven more minutes of sleep. It used to be ten, but now it's only seven—probably some conspiracy by the manufacturers to get people to eventually wake up on time, so they'll be pissed enough to buy a new clock radio. I also know that, bleary-eyed from sleep, if I stand up, turn right, take eight steps forward and then make two left turns, I'll be in my bathroom. This stuff means a lot. Being launched into the waking world is abrupt enough that you come to love the things you don't have to worry about to help you start the day.

So when I stepped into the shower after I'd cranked on the hot water for about ten seconds before it actually got hot, I wasn't prepared for the loud "bam" my shower door made as the latch hit the frame. It usually made a light "ping" sound as the spring-released lever locked into place.

My eyes flew open. Maybe my grip was off. I pulled the door toward me harder. The resounding rebellious bam that greeted me reverberated off the tiles of my shower stall and startled me into an unmistakably unsleepy condition.

What the heck was the problem? With the foolishness of the person who tries to make a non-English speaker understand English, I repeated my gesture, only louder, over and over again until I heard my neighbor stamp her feet upstairs. I stopped. Then bammed it again a few more times to make sure it wouldn't shut. But it was time to stop denying. My shower door was broken.

I peered through the water still pelting me to see that, for some reason, the latch was about a half-inch off of where it should have been. It's these moment that make me realize I am not detective material. Because I was content with that explanation of a freak occurrence for the time being. After all, much life seemed to be ordered around freak occurrences anyway, so this was no different. I spent the next ten minutes showering smashed up against the far wall with the shower head pointed away from the door so I wouldn't get the floor wet.

It wasn't until several hours later that I seriously delved into this problem of the suddenly ill-fitting shower door. Could the metal have expanded in the heat of the last few days? Or maybe the screws on the latch had gotten loose, causing it to tilt downward. Now that I thought about it, the door didn't even seem to swing right on its hinges. Yes, there was a bit more tension in it than usual. After several minutes of repeating these two-and-a-half possibilities, a third finally dawned on me: Could it be that the entire house had shifted? That was it! The house had shifted down about a half-inch or so. Hadn't I seen cracks in the wall when I first moved in? At the time, I didn't think they were a big deal. After you've lived in Los Angeles, home of the 6.7 Northridge temblor that collapsed the 10 Freeway, cracks aren't so bad. They're as common as silicone breasts at a Beverly Hills restaurant. But five years had passed. And maybe while I hit my snooze button day after day and shuffled down the hall, stepping into the bathroom and cranking on the hot water before I closed the shower door after me, those cracks had seeped their way down to the foundation, splintering a millimeter at a time, until one large chunk of the house would suddenly crumble away from the rest and the whole structure, unable to withstand this sudden secession, would come crashing down in ruins.

I was a dead woman.

And when I got home, I was a dead woman with proof.

I hadn't been imagining, because there they were. Long diagonal cracks in my shower stall. Crooked black fissures in the concrete near the ceiling. Menacing gaps by the kitchen door. Hairline crevices on my bedroom wall. Their twins were on the outside walls of the house. I imagined that, if I pushed hard enough, I could knock a whole section of my apartment down.

How had I not noticed that the walls were falling down on me? Was it that I refused to look, preferring the sight of the things that were familiar, comfortable, and reliable? My "I Love NY" coffee mug, the fold-out futon couch where I did all my reading, my hip-hop teddy bear? I knew the cracks were there but if I just looked elsewhere, I could imagine that my life was one big scale, one side which held the cracks, the other side, all the things I loved and could count on. It should be obvious who wins. But the mistake I made, the thing that would put an end to me, was forgetting the cracks were ever there. Or that they could get bigger and wider and deeper. Until one day your shower door doesn't close and there you are smashed up against the wall just trying to pretend that everything's okay.

The thing is, I knew those cracks were there. Cracks are everywhere. I thought about cracks all the time. I thought about them on the verge of sleep, or wrote about them in poems because they wouldn't fit into everyday conversation. I wrote about them in line breaks and stanzas because I couldn't talk about them in sentences. It was only in line breaks and stanzas that I could say things like,

> There are no straps on this chair,
> but if I started running
> the evening would set
> and a spotlight would follow my fleeing form
> with shots slinging past my vulnerable flesh.
> I would hit the wall with the speed of my fear
> stretching high for the bricks from whose stone razors grow
> like angry children you reach to embrace
> though you know they will cut
> your skin to the bone
> your screams from your throat

while the blood starts to flow between you like glue.
Over the wall is a dream like freedom
that pushes me through and locks you deep
where I can forget
how your words slam like jail cells
I didn't
I never
each sound from your lips like the turn of a key
that leaves me alone in inviolable walls
I've begun to call home.
The bond between us ties and restrains me,
my hands and feet numb and choked
'cause the blood doesn't flow,
our blood doesn't flow.
You live for a chamber of glass
where the mist swirls deadly and sweet on your tongue
in the pipe and your lungs
eclipsing your heart
as you breathe and suck
small burning crystals like jewels on display.
And me, I swallow time like silence,
where it sits in my stomach and waits to expel
to make room for the nothing I say to you.
Each time I leave or break these bonds,
you aim for my heart
my Achilles' heel,
and I let you shoot and kill me again,
where I rise just to serve you my love with dollars,
love to feed your blood with poison,
love you tell me keeps you alive.
And we dance like this, my rise and your fall,
your fall and my fall,
'til we drag ourselves down and let it all go,
not you and not me,

not I and not you,
but need and needed.
Like a fool I believe each time is the last,
that the causal equation is simple and true:
if I walk, you stop;
if you stop, this thing comes between us
is memory, departed
and this prison will crumble in ash and repentance
and I can call you mine again.
But my heart is full of holes from your need
and the blood pours out faster than I can hold.
And this bandage of guilt,
the bondage of need wraps tighter, constricting
choking and binding
deforming and twisting the thing inside
your creation, your prize
my defeat, the demise of what made me care in the first place.
So it's you or me,
I or you,
'cause you and I burned away,
exhaled from your lips where it disappeared, quiet as air.
There are no straps on this chair,
so I'm hitting that wall with the speed of my fear
passing through those blades with my heart in my hand
where it's safe and warm,
beating like time to recover its shape.
In my figure receding,
you'll see the hole where my heart once was,
and say that I'm cold,
unfeeling and cruel.
See, the guards don't change how they beat the captive,
so you take away the things they know:
the places that bruise, the smell of your fear.
So the one place you'll aim for

is where you can't hurt me;
the gap in my chest that you call betrayal
when I know better,
I know where my heart is:
in the hand of the person
who knows how to love.

I hid the cracks from view because I was afraid they'd make me look weak, like I couldn't stand on my own, or that my ability to stand was uncertain, unpredictable. I thought others wouldn't want to be too close in case I fell because the cracks I had were big, bigger than anyone would have ever suspected. I thought everyone would rather see the "I Love NY" coffee mug, my futon couch, my hip-hop teddy bear. That way, no one would have to bother asking about the things threatening to come crashing down on me.

And that way, I could make the mistake of forgetting that maybe those things could.

For the next two nights, I slept in the living room, the part of my house that was safe. And I surprised myself by sleeping well. But in the morning, my hand reached out to smack a coffee table, not an alarm clock, and in my disorientation, I fumbled around with the objects closest at hand, trying to figure out which was my cell phone so I could turn off the alarm. The walk to the shower was longer, painful in its delay of my everyday routine, and by the time I got to the unclosing shower door, my day had already begun as a series of small misfortunes. And I figured, this is how it was going to be. This is what life with cracks was like.

It took so long for the contractor to come to the house to inspect the foundations that I didn't even care what he had to say anymore. I'd come to think of his assessment as a death sentence, a confirmation of what I already knew. I imagined that inside of a month, I'd be packing my belongings, moving to a new apartment, and watching the place I'd called home crumble to the ground, a useless and unsalvageable pile of rubble.

And so when he said it, I thought he was lying. The house was fine, he assured me. The cracks were completely normal, something you saw in a lot of houses. Almost all of them, eventually. The ground had shifted, true, and with it, the house, but the foundation was solid. There was nothing to worry about.

He even fixed my shower door.

The next morning, when my alarm went off, I slapped my arm down towards the nightstand to hit the snooze button. But instead of going back to sleep, I kept my eyes open, letting them adjust to the dark. And when I was ready to wake up, I navigated myself forward, this time out of necessity instead of habit. The shower door didn't make that "bam" sound anymore; but neither did it make the old "ping" I was used to. The sound it made as it latched into place was something new and unfamiliar. But the door stayed closed. And as I stood there in the middle of my shower with the water running down over my head, it felt like for the first time, cracks and all, everything was going to be all right.

Tides

Water makes no promise to the shore.
You approach, knowing that
just as you come, you must recede.
It has always been like this,
this movement closer and then away again,
and each time you sweep across the shore,
sand shifts, dancing in your wake.
The tides have brought wave upon wave,
and in moments I have sought the swell.
It would not do to hold you here—
flood destroys as much as drought.
Instead, I look for the tide to turn,
knowing that just as I hold the weight of water,
you carry with you grains of sand.

Fix

Once upon a time we crept into the storage room and you kissed me behind dusty records and took an earring from my ear saying you wanted to keep it because it'd been inside of me and we cut out of work and ran to my car where we kept the whiskey but you said *I want to go higher let's go higher* so we drove to see Ronnie and I watched the snow fall before us cleaned into lines as you said *I need you I need you* like I was your fix and the next summer I came back and waited for you to say something and I thought that you might but you didn't just that we should meet up sometime and when you waved goodbye that's when I saw them that's when I saw bruises bloom on your arms.

Na Ganda

Nancy didn't really have to use the restroom, but she got up and left anyway, not wanting to witness any more of the bartender's flirting with Daniel in a language she couldn't understand. Thankfully, the toilets in the hwajangsil were not the squat kind, but the freezing temperature, green fluorescent lighting, and cold metal doors were a shock for her, having just come from the plush, dimly-lit second-floor bar with floor-to-ceiling windows. They'd chosen it because it was called "Blues Club," but inside, silky Korean pop ballads floated over the candlelit tables, well-coiffed heads, and the untouched piano in the middle of the floor.

The other patrons were dressed in the usual Seoul flair, the women in stiletto boots and off-the-shoulder sweater dresses belted tightly at the waist, the men in well-tailored button-down shirts and slacks despite the snowy weather outside. In comparison, she looked like one of the poor ajumma vendors hawking goods outside of Namdaemun market in her jeans, thick sweater, and heavy down parka, not to mention her knit cap, scarf, and mittens. Walking around the city, she had gotten used to the dismissive sniffs and blatant staring of the more fashionable women around her, provoking her to grimace and think, *At least I'm not going to freeze to death because I'm too vain to* wear something *in the middle of fucking winter*. In the bar, it was no different. The hostess had looked her up and down, making clear her disapproval one second before sweetly asking her and Daniel how many people would be in their party.

Daniel knew how important appearance—"suh-tyle"—was to Koreans, knew that it determined how nicely others treated you, how good the service would be, even how much something might cost, so he dressed warmly, but in cashmere, wool, and leather gloves, keeping his lines clean and tailored, unlike hers. As he glided across the shiny wood floor of the bar, Nancy could see the shape of his torso under his sweater. She, on the other hand, had forgotten what her body looked like under so many layers of clothing, and had begun to think she no longer had one.

Nancy lingered in the restroom. She washed her hands, darting them in and out of the water since the faucet ran cold. Her fingertips numbed. She shook them off and tucked them under her armpits, but the pressure only squeezed the chill into her flesh. Her eyes and nose were red. This, with her pale skin, gave her the look of a junkie. She wasn't cut out for cold weather, wasn't one of those girls who could trounce around with curled hair and a mini-skirt in mid-December. On the city streets, she could only concentrate on how not to freeze to death, the wind piercing her skin like thousands of icy daggers.

She took off her cap and tried to fluff her hair, now matted against her skull. She'd gotten it cut into a short bob soon after coming to Seoul, having discovered that the combination of hard water and low-watt hair dryers gave her stick-straight hair no matter what she did to it. The strands clung to her fingers like kite strings from the static electricity, then snapped back down against the flat sheet of her hair.

The hostess had led them to one of the tables near the windows. Nancy slid into the booth, eager to watch the snow falling over the small city street below. Icy flakes drifted over the large windows and softened the bright yellow and red neon signs. She sighed at the prettiness of it. Sometimes, she really did feel that she was on a set of a beautifully romantic Korean drama. But her reverie didn't last. The waitress, a reed-thin woman with immaculate skin, wearing her glossy long hair pulled back neatly into a ponytail, addressed her—an insult, because it meant that she thought Nancy was the elder on the table—and asked what she would like.

In the company of other non-Korean-speaking friends, Nancy might've struggled in her elementary Korean to correct the mistake, but since Daniel was there, she hung back, relieved, expecting him to take the lead. After all, having spent his childhood years in Seoul, he was fluent in Korean. In the two days since his arrival, he'd handled all their interactions—taxi rides, ordering at restaurants, even reading labels at the supermarket—with an effortlessness she cherished more than envied. She had begun to think of his one-week visit as *her* vacation, her break from all the misinterpretations each moment living in Seoul had brought her. But when the waitress asked her, "Annyeonhasimnikka, mwol deurilkkayo?" Daniel said nothing, putting his elbows on the table, resting his clasped hands against his lips. Nancy cocked her head, confused. Discomfited by the silence, she turned back to the waitress and asked for a wine list, the words tripping out of her mouth like rocks.

As Nancy had predicted, when she couldn't speak Korean properly, the waitress addressed her in Japanese. "No. Miguk-saram ye yo," Nancy muttered. The waitress covered her mouth, laughing nervously, and with a babyish lilt in her voice, apologized and ran off, presumably, to find someone who could speak English.

As soon as the waitress was out of earshot, Nancy turned to Daniel.

"Why didn't you say anything?" Daniel shrugged his shoulders and sat across her, his gaze observant.

The bathroom smelled faintly of urine. She had never gotten used to the fact that she wasn't supposed to flush toilet paper here because the city sewer systems weren't built to process large amounts of paper waste. She figured she was just one foreigner who ignored the rules—surely the system could handle that—but then again, she wasn't the only foreigner who ignored the rules. They all did. Weston, one of the many Canadian ex-pats she worked with teaching English at the hagwon, routinely insisted on sitting in the nearly always-empty seats in the subway cars reserved for pregnant women, old people, and the handicapped. Maybe because he was a foreigner and definitely because he was black, no one ever chastised him. Once on a crowded train ride when she protested his dragging her up front onto the empty seat next to him, he'd said glibly, "Honey, we *are* handicapped. We can't speak the language. Sit *down*." Nancy had spent the whole ride avoiding the looks of the other passengers, who she knew most likely thought that she and Weston were dating, and because he was black, most likely thought she was loose.

I am handicapped, Nancy mused. It frustrated her that she still couldn't speak the language after five months in Seoul. She knew that in Weston's case, laziness was to blame, but she, like the other foreign-born Koreans she had met, labored each day to put simple sentences together. Maybe it was true that hangeul was an emotional language, virtually inaccessible to those, like her, who felt they would never be Korean enough.

Nancy's hands were still cold. She punched the button on the hand dryer. More cold air blew out of the vents.

Before she could continue, another waitress—who could have been the other woman's sister—approached their table and bowed to Nancy, attempting to take her order in English. Nancy gave up correcting the mistake in her age and asked for wine—she'd learned quickly that in most bars, Koreans were awful at mixed drinks—but the waitress knit her thin, arched brows and responded, "This table for food. You eat food?"

Of course I eat food, Nancy thought. She glanced again at Daniel, who was still sitting with his clasped hands against his mouth. Nancy turned back to the waitress's halting English. Eventually, she figured out that they couldn't sit at the window booths or tables unless they were planning to order some kind of banchan. Patrons who came to drink were relegated to the curved wooden bar near the front entrance.

Nancy scanned the room. There were several other window booths open, and the bar wasn't crowded. She didn't want to move. But just as she began to protest, Daniel cut her off with

"Ne, algeseoyo," and the next thing she knew, the woman, giggling profusely, had taken Daniel's arm and was leading him across the room. Nancy scuttled out of the booth and followed them towards the bar. As Daniel slipped onto one of the stools, he and the waitress bowed several times to each other as he repeated, "Algeseoyo, gwaenchanayo," and the waitress continued to giggle. Nancy felt the urge to yank the woman by her hair and slap her. Daniel looked over his shoulder at Nancy and with a jerk of his head, motioned for her to sit with him.

She knew the other patrons probably weren't staring, but she couldn't shake the feeling that they were. She plopped herself onto the seat to Daniel's left and threw her purse unceremoniously on the floor. She still felt like striking the waitress, but turned to Daniel instead.

"You know," she started. But he'd already begun chatting with the bartender, a slip of a girl who barely looked old enough to drink.

"Na ganda," Nancy practiced in front of the mirror. She knew it was all in the tone, that her volume and inflection made the difference between a simple statement and an indignant response. She tried to recall scenes from some of the dramas she'd watched in which the women characters, retaining with steel clutches every fragment of their shattered pride, took their exits from thoughtless lovers.

"Na, ganda," she repeated forcefully. Her voice echoed and Nancy suddenly worried that someone might be in the hall, might have heard her recitation. When did she become such a spaz? She ran the phrase over in her head a few more times before she realized that she had been rehearsing in Korean. Why did she need to say that she was leaving in Korean? For the bartender's sake? The bartender knew she was a foreigner. Why humiliate herself by uttering something she probably wasn't pronouncing correctly anyway? The thought of the bartender's dark, bouncy curls only inflamed Nancy's anger—the way they'd spilled over the girl's shoulders as she bobbed her head giggling at Daniel. Nancy knew Daniel was handsome. In fact, seeing him here made her more aware of his beauty. In Hawai'i, he was good-looking, but a little too pale, a little too lean, a little too FOB. He didn't quite dress right. But here, he was gorgeous. And from the way he smiled at the bartender, his eyes shining, Nancy saw that he knew it. So much so that he hadn't seemed to notice when, after the bartender laughed at something he'd said, putting one hand over her mouth and placing the other on top of his hand, Nancy slid off her barstool and left.

Nancy faced the mirror.

"I'm leaving," she said. Her tone was dry, cold, and discomfiting, like the air.

Nancy's nearly full wineglass rested on the bar apart from Daniel and the bartender. She headed for it, a lighthouse for her course, straightening her posture and mustering up the most graceful walk she could manage given that she wore hiking boots. Daniel leaned forward on his elbows, speaking animatedly. The bartender's fingers pressed against her lips as her laugh pierced the air. In front of Daniel was a drawing of map and a phone number written neatly on a cocktail napkin. Nancy slipped onto her barstool, lifted her glass, and took a sip of her Malbec, placing it back down and sliding it next to Daniel's elbow. A few moments later, he lifted his arm in gesture, spilling wine over the bar.

"Ah!" the bartender gasped, zipping towards the spill with a towel. The deep plum color seeped into the white cloth.

Daniel reached over the bar and grabbed a stack of small square cocktail napkins, wiping what he could. Nancy sat with her hands folded in her lap.

The bartender and Daniel continued to laugh, speaking in Korean.

Nancy took a breath, hoisting her purse over her shoulder.

"I'm leaving," she enunciated.

"What? Where are you going?" Daniel paused, the wet napkins in his hand, his face marked by leftover laughter from his conversation with the bartender.

"I said, I'm leaving. What's the matter—don't speak English?"

Nancy met his gaze, then turned abruptly and headed for the door.

It wasn't until she was halfway down the street that Daniel caught up with her. He yanked her elbow roughly.

"What was that about?"

Nancy smiled sweetly. "What was what about?"

Daniel buttoned his coat, his bare fingers fumbling. *So he is cold*, Nancy thought.

"Leaving?" He dug in his pockets and pulled out his gloves.

"Bar sucked. I can't help it if you have no taste. Then again, you did grow up here."

Nancy glanced down the street at the Hyundae Mini-Mart that was next to the subway station entrance. The convenience store's white and teal neon sign anchored her in the swirling snow. Pulling her cap low and adjusting her scarf over her nose and mouth, she headed for the sign, her hiking boots digging assuredly down into the sidewalk.

Daniel ran after her, skidding slightly as he came up around her side.

"It's freezing. Why don't we just wait at the bar until the snow lets up?"

Nancy pulled her scarf down so she could speak. "Why don't you wait at the bartender's house until the snow lets up?"

"What are you talking about?"

Nancy whipped off her mittens, then shoved her hands into the pockets of Daniel's coat. He pulled away and they struggled for a moment before she felt the napkin in her fingers and yanked it out.

"This!" She thrust the napkin in Daniel's face. "You think

because I can't speak Korean I'm blind? That slut gave this to you, right?" She balled up the napkin and tossed it into the street. She expected Daniel to lurch after it, but he didn't. Instead, he stood looking at her, a gleam of triumph in his eyes.

"You know what that was?"

The question wasn't rhetorical. He really expected an answer. Tired of standing in the snow, Nancy replied, "The address of a whorehouse?"

"I told her my girlfriend liked jazz, so she gave me the name of a good club we could go to."

"Yeah, right."

Daniel exhaled, exasperated. "You're psycho."

"Fine. This psycho's going home. You can stay with the whore."

Nancy repositioned her scarf again so that only her eyes were exposed and resumed her trek towards the subway station. She was halfway there before she heard the light crunching of Daniel's steps behind her.

The subway station was only slightly warmer than it was outside. Chilled air blew through the tunnels with a hollow whistle. Nancy was fixed on the large digital screen mounted against one of the pillars separating the tracks, watching commercials for vitamin drinks. Tall, thin girls with no muscle tone wore tiny shorts and tank tops as they jogged through the park, hair and makeup flawless, outrunning even more beautiful men with looks of astonishment on their faces as the women sped by.

Daniel stood next to her, shifting his weight back and forth. She knew he'd say something eventually, but until then, was content contemplating the irony of a country that obsessed about health but felt muscles and muscle tone were tacky and unattractive.

Daniel exhaled loudly. "Maybe this wasn't such a good idea."

The next commercial flashed on the screen.

"I can look up some old friends and stay with them. I was planning to look them up anyway," he continued.

Nancy watched a woman with an updo, pearl earrings, and a silk wrap dress cleaning her house furiously and looking nervously at a clock. Dejected, the woman suddenly brightened after remembering she had a vitamin drink in her refrigerator.

"Nancy. You going to talk to me?" She felt his hand on her arm. She shook it off.

"You want to talk?" Nancy noticed an older man in a suit and scarf, listening to them, mostly likely trying to piece their conversation together. "Okay, talk."

Daniel followed her gaze to the ajeosshi, then turned back to her. "I don't think you want me here. You're different here. I don't know."

Nancy shot a look at the man. They locked stares before he narrowed his eyes angrily then looked away.

"I'm the same. You're the one who's different."

Daniel ran his hand through his hair. "This place is making you different. You never talk like this."

"No, *you* never talk like this."

"Keep your voice down."

"I'm not shouting. Besides, like anyone even cares what we're talking about." She turned back to the screen.

Announcing the approaching train, a woman's voice chimed out of the speakers, first in Korean, then in English. Nancy moved behind the yellow line marking the subway door's position. Daniel followed her.

The train screeched on its tracks. Nancy turned to Daniel.

"Where was the club?"

"What?"

"The club?"

Daniel paused. "Hyewha."

"What was it called?"

"I don't remember. She wrote the number down in case we got lost."

They crammed into the subway car crowded mostly with

students and tired ajummas and ajeosshis. Her train wasn't headed towards Gangnam, the newer, fashionable part of the city with brightly-lit cafes and upscale European boutiques. Hers would snake through Gangbuk, the oldest parts of Seoul, the parts that survived the war. Two halmeonis sat in the reserved seats up front, their fingerless-gloved hands folded on their bellies, their heads hanging forward as they slept. Large packages tied up in bright handkerchiefs sat at their feet. The seats across from them were empty.

Nancy let her weight drop forward, gripping the plastic hand-loop that kept her from toppling over each time the train jolted. The announcements asking passengers to stay clear of the doors as they opened and closed looped endlessly, with a short segment of Vivaldi's "Spring," then the Korean announcement, then the English, then back again, over and over.

They didn't make love that night.

She didn't need to search his pockets to know the napkin was there.

The next morning, Nancy got up and showered while Daniel lay in bed, watching Korean game shows. She had a private lesson to teach at nine.

The weather outside cast a dull grey pallor over the city. Nancy dressed slowly, layer upon layer. She turned to Daniel who had buried himself in the sheets. He didn't look at her.

"Na ganda," she said.

A Toast
–for Marisa

In search of the finer things,
you and I in a small white Toyota
wind our way up the 29
and pop in the Cocteau Twins
when the radio cuts out.
On this day we celebrate our
nondependence.
In the photograph,
we ponder over fields of
fragrant vine, only to find
that the scent is not grape,
but rose.
A decoy, the guide tells us,
to fend off
the destructive feeding of insects.

Tipsy from wine and
grumpy from heat,
we slump under meager shade,
lunching on salmon and cheese.
Our pictures display
smiles and abandon,
yet sandwiched between
a thin coat of film and
the memory of this day
is the sadness from which we run.
We layer our tongues
with wines sweet and bitter;
with each sip our palates dull,
coated thick with essence of wood,

flower, and berry.
We deny our drunkenness
the way we forget our pain,
let this glass of wine
lure us with its sweetness
away from what causes us to drink,
inhale the intoxicating warmth of rose
while tender fruit ages and ripens
under an unforgiving sun.

자기 확장

Doing Gender

I never learned gender.
The gift my mama gave me was pushing me out of the kitchen
where I didn't really want to be in the first place,
in that space of sharp staccato and pungent steam,
nimble fingers and the whoosh of the refrigerator door
sucking itself open and closed,
the clank and clattering,
the intermittent torrential bursts of sound
that roared each morning and settled down each evening
like an engine slowly rotating to a stop,
a place I heard ringing through the house
for most of my childhood moments
that I spent reading on my bed
or on the couch,
my legs thrown over the back,
my world a place of curious girls solving crimes
and misfit children battling wizards,
of grail quests and travels through time,
those days I read stories over and over and over
because each page in my hand reminded me of possibility,
the same possibility that pushed me out of the kitchen
and out the front doors onto roller skates,
asphalt, grass, and sand,
where I learned there was something bigger than this house,
and I learned there was something more than me.

It was her hands, those mama hands that fed me each day
that pushed me out of the kitchen when
women hands, auntie hands, father hands pushed me in.
It was her hands, those mama hands that pushed me out of the
kitchen

because she wanted me to feed myself with something besides
chopped vegetables and seasoned meat, something besides
glistening grains and sliced fruit.
She wanted me to feed the world with something besides
what could be boiled, steamed, fried, baked, marinated,
stewed, tossed, or whipped.
She wanted me to love.

And there is love in a kitchen.
There is love in women's talk
and love in the church of the home where women preach.
There is love in the questions and comparisons,
the stories and suggestions and proclamations
that tenderize meat and sweeten glazes,
wash dark leaves and drain pearled rice.

There is love in that place that drives the home.

But she wanted me to love in all the ways a woman can love:
love beyond dishes, love beyond taste,
love beyond Band-Aids and fussing,
love beyond this body.
She wanted me to love with words,
with vision,
with deeds and bravery,
with the belief there was nothing I could not do,
nothing I *had* to do.
She wanted me to talk out, not back.
She wanted me to sing.
She wanted me to live
beyond this thing called "girl,"
this thing that divides,
trains us to live half a life,
denies the fullness of soul that pushed us here into this world.

She wanted me to understand all the things a human is—
emotional and rational,
delicate and aggressive,
feeling and thinking,
nurturing and leading,
so she took her mama hands and pushed me out of the kitchen,
that holy place at whose altar she worshipped three times each day,
pushed me out of the temple
and past doctrine
into the world to find my god.

And I found my god
in spaces with two separate doors,
in well-lit rooms that pretended democracy,
in public places whose invisible fences barbed.
I found my god in elevated pulpits
whose hidden stairs I climbed
with mama hands pushing at my shoulders like wings,
stood at the pulpit and gazed at crowds
knowing that it was time to speak the speech of a woman,
time to speak the speech of a soul.

So there, on the pulpit,
I preached of love and injustice,
of broken children and fallen soldiers,
of stolen land and angry women,
of language lost and presidents who lie,
of victims who struggle to resuscitate hope,
of all the things I wanted to say
and I spoke the speech that comes from a woman,
and I spoke the speech that comes from a soul
to harmonize with the speech of her cutting and washing and
chopping and frying
and countless fingers dipped in to taste what she knew would nourish

and that gift she gave me by double-timing her labor instead of
dividing the burden to share with me—
the choice to beat in the heart of the kitchen;
the choice to feed with the food of the soul.

Angry Women

It's not the first time I've heard it, that
women are crazy—
that unlike guys, who'll get into fist fights
then buy each other beer,
we hold grudges.
It's also not the first time I've heard that
it's much better to piss off a guy
than a woman because women?
Women are mean.
Translation:
Hell hath no fury like a woman scorned.
It's nothing new,
these attitudes, these platitudes
all telling us we've got no right to get mad,
and if we do, we're doing it wrong.
When we wanna say that something's not right,
they tell us
with women the heart argues, not the mind.
In other words, we're not logical enough
to go around clocking each other
whenever we've got bones to pick.
First of all,
when was the last time you told a girl
it was okay to deck someone when she was upset?
You can't take away a woman's fists
then punish her for using the things she's got left,
like her words,
her feelings,
and her power of eternal memory.
Would you really prefer that we make you bleed?
As if the world doesn't have enough of that.

See, every twenty seconds here in paradise,
a woman gets hit.
And every three seconds here on Earth,
she's beaten, raped, or killed.
So maybe we're too damn tired of it
to inflict it on someone else.
And besides,
anger is anger
and maybe you should
question the source,
not assign it a gender.
I see angry men starting wars,
killing our children,
and destroying our Earth.
But I also see angry men
marching for peace,
shouting for justice,
and surviving their fear.
And maybe all I want is the right
to get mad at the wrongs in our world
without being called those things meant to shut me up:
like hysterical, irrational, illogical, psychotic,
man-hater, male-basher, feminazi, or bitch.
When I think of anger that comes from sisters,
I think of anger that comes from love,
of Nigerian woman workers
on strike at Chevron-Texaco,
demanding jobs for their sons,
schools and hospitals for their town;
of Dolores Huerta,
founding UFW,
getting rights for farm workers
when she saw their kids
going to school without shoes;

of Iraqi women visiting Colin Powell
to insist on health care and human rights;
of Joanna Macy, who testified at the
World Uranium Hearings to plead for the
protection of earth from the "poison fire";
of Wilma Mankiller who united the Cherokee Nation
one-hundred-fifty-seven years after the Trail of Tears;
of Mililani Trask who studied the rules of the system
so she could fight it to help all Indigenous people;
and of Kim Hak-sun who broke a forty-year silence
to talk of her rapes during World War II,
then sued Japan's government in a call for justice
to comfort her fellow sexual slaves.
Maybe Lord Byron got it right when he said
sweet is revenge—especially to women.
Because the things we avenge are the crimes that
transcend time,
transcend nations,
and yes, transcend, this battle of sexes,
because *a free race cannot be born of slave mothers,*
and all of us here, we all come from our mothers,
and so yes, our revenge is sweet
and yes, we hold grudges
as our way of saying we will not forget
how you destroy our children,
and send them to die for money,
we will not forget these things that hurt you
as they hurt ourselves
because all we want,
all we want is a little bit of peace,
a little respect,
a little safety for this traumatized world.
So the next time you face an angry woman,
make the effort to see what causes her pain,

knowing that we, like you, reserve the right to get mad
for any number of a thousand stupid reasons.
But if she asks that you see her as a human being,
and if she will not raise her fists to say
that she will not stand for your denying her right to be your peer,
then show her you know how to speak her language
and hear her words for the sake of their speech
knowing *a bird doesn't sing because it*
has an answer;
it sings because
it has a song.

For the Uncolored Colored Girls

The first time she jabs me, I shed a tear;
the second time,
I twist her wrist, seize the offending tool,
watch her purple lips hiss
You need some color,
her coffee brown fingers waving admonishing circles
at my pale toneless canvas.
Her prescription hangs like a sentence
sinks like a curtain
and the show begins
as she orchestrates lip gloss, bronzers, shadow, and mirrors
her minions in missions to save the plain,
crushing her brush into pots of pigment,
then grinding hostile hues into my flesh.
Each sable hair stabs like a needle
invading my pores
tattooing my skin with her cure to my
tragic lack of melanin.

You can take the girl out of the shade,
but you can't change the shade of the girl:
I am pale, fair, light, porcelain, linen,
vellum, vanilla, fair light, neutral light,
cream, cloud, ivory, light ivory, nude ivory, and tint 001.
I am not toffee, caramel, suede, cocoa, or truffle.
I am not even beige.

To remedy this malady
Ms. Toasted Pecan paints me scalp to chin,
bruises my lids ash purple,
lines my eyes kohl black,

flushes my cheeks orgasm peach,
sparkles my lips mauve splash,
but when I go home,
these colors will stain my shirt, smear my sheets,
wash down the drain with the rest of the dirt
and all there'll be left is where I began,
you know,
needing some color.

I want to tell Madame Makeover
how I get asked if I speak English though I've got a PhD;
how, for the Vietnam war, vets apologize to me;
how I've been congratulated for writing like those popular oriental ladies—
you know me—
fast tracking my way to broadcast news,
serving my man and giggling like geisha,
submitting and obeying like it's my true nature.

Seems to me I got plenty of color.

And if you don't believe that,
ask the women who sew in a dark, squalid room
so a teenage girl can dress for her prom,
and the women who sell their bodies online
to faraway masters with American names,
and the bargirls who let you slide your hand up their thighs
when you've got enough money and it's pussy you buy.
Seems it ain't so much color as it is the blood
and my blood runs dark, heavy, and real.

If you ask me, cream and coffee mix fine,
like the palest of cheese and the darkest of wine
And whoever says never the two shall meet

unless it's in an alley on opposite street sides
is hoping it all ends like this:
us fisting it out over lipstick and gloss,
while we forget the broken backs
and the unpaid costs of the toil
of our mothers and sisters and brothers and children
whose fingers paint dollars and minutes,
rubbing tired eyes and dressing wounds,
whose color is measured not in gradient but strength,
packaged by lineage and not by brand,
whose skin wears the mark not of style but survival,
and whose hands seek truth and not what conceals.

El Vato Loco

El Vato Loco walked into my classroom
he didn't have a pencil or paper,
he didn't have any books
just a thoughtful gaze and a crouching slouch
when he sat in his desk, like he might have to fly.
I never knew his gang name;
to me he was Phil, the letters that spelled out his
junior college, non-esé identity
wearing a long trail of zeros and slashes,
'cause though he came every day like school was his church
he gave me nothing on paper,
no records or proof that he had been there.
One day I walked in to his empty chair
and halfway through class,
the soft rapid-fire of a knock at the door
took me into the hall where I saw him bruised,
the cleaned-up wounds where blood used to be
the swelling and sadness of la vida loca's embrace.
He had come to apologize for his absence that day,
and told me, he promised, he'd be back.

I never saw him again.

He fell through the cracks, probably into his grave.
this vato from East L.A. who thought
if he couldn't become a college grad
let him at least become El Veterano,
the one who lived.
The schools have changed, the zip codes, the states,
but year after year, they keep on falling,
the single mothers who study during lunch breaks at work,

the teenagers who go straight from night shift to class,
the ex-cons whose tats peek out from their sleeves,
the laid-off workers trying to feed their kids.
The recovering addicts on borrowed time,
the daughters and sons left to raise the rest,
the girls with TROs out on their exes,
the boys fathering babies with their high school girlfriends.
The good life stretches before them like fields
they can only cross in small degrees,
finishing class, finishing years,
but the gap stretches wide held open by hands
that blame the poor for their poverty,
the colored for racism,
the women for rape,
the victims for war;
tell you who to love
and who you can't marry,
what to do with your body,
and whom you should fear.
The gap stretches wide to keep on swallowing,
the survivors forgetting the cost of survival,
and the ones who remember can only reach down so far
before what felt like a handshake becomes fingers outstretched
like invisible strings could bring back the dead.
How do you close a gap that keeps stretching?
Do you make a bridge of willing survivors,
or lower each other down for the rescue?
Or do you wait 'til the bodies fill the gap so we cross their backs
to the other side?

When I close my eyes,
my world looks like this:
we care for ourselves and help when we can;
we love who we want and pray without judgment;

we're happy when those around us succeed;
and El Vato Loco turns in his homework.
You close the gap by fighting the hands
whose life work it is to keep it wide
and make sure that the hands that keep it wide
sure as hell ain't the ones you call your own.

The Little Things

Sometimes it's the little things that do you in
the small cuts you give yourself each day,
cold metal on shivering skin
that weeps like tears releasing the push
of the thing inside that grows like a tumor barely contained
subdues the parts that want to live
'til you forget they were ever there
and all you feel
is how you and the pain
are twins from one mother
connected and cursed to the single fate
of giving up.
So you carve those lines across your flesh
erasing how
you used to laugh without disguise
used to kiss without transaction
used to trust the ones who bore you
'til they drilled their anger through your heart
and left you like an unstrung bead whose cord's been cut,
no link to show you that you belong—
and so you don't.

Instead you tally injuries in scores and marks
upon your arms
bleeding lines inside your thighs
until you wear
your life's story
the sting of razors little things
against the hurt you keep inside
that seeps its way up to your flesh
writes its shape in dark brown scars

like cryptic letters you decode
each time you lie in bed at night,
your fingers having memorized
the length and slant of every gash,
the lines like chains that sentence you
to a lifetime term
to each unkind word
and undeserved slap,
each unwanted kiss
and blind accusation
'til you forget you used to be
a girl who owned the skin around her,
who only dreamed of lines that came from age
that came from wisdom,
who wrapped herself in who she was
'til they cut you down,
piece by piece,
little by little.

Sometimes you take the blade and push
to find the limits of your living,
that line between your life and death
held in resistant walls of veins
that stop the steel from going further
with nothing more than the simple act
of pushing back.

But it's that little thing of pushing back
that keeps you on this side of life
because living things prefer to go on living
and somewhere lodged inside your pain
is a tiny seed called survival
that holds its own
even when the pressure comes

even when the pain is closing in
it knows the difference between
giving in and giving up
and it's this little thing that's called survival
that keeps the blade from slicing through
that keeps you here tied to the world,
tied to belonging.

And you are not a little thing,
and you are not a little thing.

You are not a little thing
and if someone tells you you're a little thing
if someone cuts you down in pieces
remember how little things
add up
how little things can
do you in
and there is no such thing as
a little thing
and you know this from your wounded arms
you know this from your broken heart
and one day when you touch those scars
and on the day age pales those stains
you'll recall the time
the rebellious spring of a resistant vein
showed this girl
the will to live was in her body—
she had it in her all along.

Goodbye Yellow Brick Road: An Ode to the High Heel

Come on, baby.
You can't say we didn't have a good ride.
We had a lot of good times together—remember all those parties,
all the clubs, those trips we took to New York, San Francisco, and
Seoul?
All those dinners, those invite-only places?
We went everywhere together—
you even came to every single one of my readings.
You been there for me all along and no matter what, I will always
love you.
See, you made me feel like a woman.
With you, I felt strong, sexy,
and you made me see the world from a whole different point of view.
You always knew how to match my moods,
and you helped me get to wherever I wanted to go.
And there's a part of me that even now wonders if I'm doing the right
thing,
but baby, the truth is,
I think it's time for us to part.
See, these days,
I want to know I'm moving forward all on my own.
I want to know what it's like to stand on my own two feet.
And no, you never did anything I didn't ask you to do,
but sometimes...it hurt to be with you.
Sometimes, because of you, I was sitting in a corner
instead of turning it up on the dance floor.
Sometimes, because of you,
I couldn't go with my friend on walks through the park
or hikes in the woods,

telling them, no, no, I'm cool, you go ahead—just so I could chill with you.
And I wonder if secretly, maybe that's where you really wanted me:
on the sidelines,
looking good,
like that's the only thing I was good for.
But you know, even though I suspected all that was true,
I was afraid to let you go because who would I be without you?
What would it look like if I showed up someplace without you?
I didn't want people looking at me,
suspicious,
thinking something wasn't right,
trying not to stare,
trying not to be rude,
wondering where you were.
It was just easier to stay with you.
But I can't, not anymore.
I can't live like this anymore,
having you determine what I do and don't do.
I want to dance until I'm breathless,
I want to run through the streets,
I want to always see the world from own my point of view.
It's time, you know, for me to be me.
So I'm sorry, but this,
this is goodbye.
I'll always remember you.
And I thank you for everything.
I'll still see you on special occasions—
you know, birthdays, Christmases, holidays.
But tell you what—don't call me;
I'll call you.
I gotta walk my own path now,
'cause you know,
Dorothy might've been the bomb on the yellow brick road,
but when she got back to Kansas,
she was who she was.

Where the Women At? or Poem for the Young Woman Who Shoved Me out of the Way at the Psychokinetics Show So She Could Shake Her Butt in Front of All the MCs

Maybe she thought I was competition,
a partition between her earth-quaking body
and her intended target,
her hips shooting arrows like Cupid on crack,
rapid fire and blazing
like only girls who practice can really do.
And practice she must have
because even after my body bounced off
neighboring biceps of the brothers around me,
I had to give it to her:
the girl could shake.

So there I was, trapped under
now-you-see-them-now-you-don't armpits
as hands waved in the air,
trying to fight my way back to the front
because I came to hear the music
and the reason I'm up front is that
I was blessed with five feet one and not a fraction more.
But Sister Shake took up the front line,
so it was me and the armpits the rest of the show.
And I can tell you: it was a smelly ride.
Maybe if I was meaner or greener,
I would've shoved her back,

but I know what it's like to be hit as a woman
and I will never raise my hand to another sister.

And besides, she was bigger than me.

So what do you do when a sister raises her hand to you?
See it wasn't the shove but the heart behind it, saying,
You are standing between me and a man
and if you don't move aside, I will move it for you.
For girls like that, we're all in the way.

So as I ducked my head side-to-side
trying to watch the show round Sister Shimmy,
I wondered, where the women at?
The ones who'd let their vertically challenged sisters
watch a show unimpeded,
who'd dance with you instead of at you,
who'd reach out to hug you tight or hold your hand,
hell, who'd take up the mic
and throw down some rhymes, put the men to shame.
You want a competition?
Let's see who can liberate our sisters faster.

Your contenders?

In this corner, visionaries like

bell hooks, Gloria Anzaldúa, Cherríe Moraga, Trinh Minh-Ha,
Grace Lee Boggs, Yuri Kochiyama, Adrienne Rich, Angela Davis

battling

Paula Gunn Allen, Audre Lorde, Hisaye Yamamoto, June Jordan,
Joy Harjo, Anna Mae Aquash, Haunani-Kay Trask, and Theresa Cha

for titles held by

Betty Friedan, Judy Baca, Janice Mirikitani, Rosa Parks,
Rigoberta Menchú, Dolores Huerta, Lili'uokalani, Alice Walker

with champs like

Monica Sone, Frida Kahlo, Winnie Mandela, Ryu Gwansun,
Ida B. Wells, Wilma Mankiller, Sojourner Truth, and Mother Jones.

The rules?
You fight your battles shaking fists, not booty,
using words sharper than knives as your weapons of choice.
When these women danced, they shook in celebration,
hands held up high like the aspirations they got from their mothers
and gave to their kin.
And while I can't say that some of that bumping and grinding
wasn't meant to conjure love sweet love,
I can guarantee that they'd have made room for their sisters
to see the show.

So to the young woman who shoved me out of the way
so she could shake her butt at all the MCs:
I'm not the enemy holding you back,
polishing your chains so they shine like gold—
and until you see me as your sister in arms,
shaking booty's as far as your freedom will go.

Bleach

Right next door to me is Crazy Eleanor, who wears a platinum blonde wig that matches her skin and makes her look like paper. She reminds me of kindergarten, of crayons gone wild, the scrawl of cornflower blue on her lids, brick red on her cheeks, sienna brown on her mouth. Colorful, but she hates color. You can tell by the way she puts it on. Angry, hateful strokes. Like she knows it has to be there, but isn't real happy about it.

When she moved in next door, she asked me if I could help her watch the plants on her porch so the Mexicans wouldn't steal them. And didn't I hate the fact that we had blacks in the building? Because she swears to God, whenever she sees one her heart just pounds, oh, she gets so scared. Did I see what *they* did in Long Beach? Shooting that cop? She loves the police. And if they're going to shoot at them, then they deserve to be beaten like that Rodney King fellow. She's a born-again Christian, did I know she loves God and Jesus? And she knows God made blacks, but she doesn't understand why they have to be so dirty. She keeps her apartment spotless, would I like to see? She's real glad that I'm Japanese (I'm not) because the Japanese are so clean. Now, she loves God and Jesus was Jewish, but she doesn't understand why the Jews are so filthy. Look, her porch is so clean I could eat off it....

And I can't help thinking that she thinks I get it. That she and I are from the same tribe. But I doubt anyone asks her if she speaks English.

Would she love me if I were dark?

I used to get teased all the time for being so pale. They said I was haole in disguise. I spent hours at the beach, baking long and slow, burning the white out of my skin. And no matter how dark I got, it was never enough. My sister told me that my mom gave birth before I was "done" and that's why I was white—because I didn't cook long enough. And my grandma was always touching my hair, so light, like hapa, not like hers, jet black even before she went grey. Someone way back must've jumped the fence.

So maybe I'm pale and maybe even haole, but I know I'm not like Crazy Eleanor.

Pretty soon she added me to her hit list. It happened after I wrote a letter of complaint to our manager because she stood in the hall one day screaming at the Taiwanese boys downstairs to go back to China where they belonged and to learn English while they were at it. Now she thinks I'm a defective oriental, a yellow girl gone wrong because I'm not polite and she swears she saw a cockroach run out of my place.

One day every week, the whole complex smells like bleach. She likes to take it by the bucket and wipe down everything in her apartment. She likes to kill off the germs, bleach the color out of her floors, her life, the world. It's the spots that drive her crazy, the damn spots, so she wears down her skin, trying to scrub them away.

Flying Blonde

I am not a natural blonde.

Despite the many oh-so-impressive surgical advances in the field of
plastic surgery,
Koreans don't come in my color, and P.S., my monolids keep it real.

But in the eleven months that I've been a blonde,
I have tried to move large furniture in my Miata,
locked myself out of the bathroom because I couldn't figure out which
way the handle turned (it didn't—you just had to push),
and wondered why I couldn't unscrew a bottle of beer that was
already open.

Did I mention I graduated from private school?

I would like to blame age or sleep deprivation for these slips of reason
and common sense,
but the truth is,
I'm not confidently sure how much these lapses of the most simple of
cognitive skills
can't be traced to the day I came home with my goldie locks,
and damn it all to hell if I said I don't giggle a helluva lot more these
days.

But on the bright side, as a truly blonde friend said in consolation:
When you're blonde, no one expects you to be smart, so when you
fuck up, it's okay.

Underestimation is not new.
I have been patted on the head for being 5'1",
instructed on how to use my tire-pressure gauge because I'm a woman,

been on the receiving end of an order of cocktails because of
my tats,
and asked if I speak English because I'm Asian—

Did I mention I got my BA from SC?

I sometimes wonder how to play to my advantage,
to let others think my knowledge of literature is limited to *People,
Us Weekly, In Touch, and Star Magazine*
just long enough to ninja their asses by talking about
postcolonial and neonationlist class and color politics of
tribal divisions
in Chimamanda Ngozi Adichie's *Half of a Yellow Sun.*

Did I mention my Master's Degree was in English?

But looks are deceiving,
and we read books by their cover,
and underestimation is nothing new—it just comes in different
colors.
And maybe if I were blonde from Sweden or Norway
people wouldn't speak to me simply
but blonde from Hawaiʻi and they think
primitive *and* dumb.

Witness once upon a time and not so long ago,
someone on the plane asked me what we used for money instead
of U.S. dollars,
and once upon a time and a little longer ago,
others asked me if I climbed a coconut tree for my dinner,
and just the other day, someone said, "You Hawaiians are just so
laid-back and carefree,"
and for the ukubillionth time, I was like,
Hawaiian is a bloodline you dumbass,
not a label you get just 'cause you live here.

(Not really: I said, Yes, I was born and raised Hawai'i, but I'm not
racially Hawaiian.
In Hawai'i, we don't say "Hawaiian" unless we mean by blood.
In fact, the delineation between what we call local and Hawaiian
is a contested arena that depends on several cultural signifiers not
excluding heritage, place, and genealogy.
Furthermore, the high cost of living and wage disparity often means
many of us hold multiple jobs.)

Did I mention I have a PhD?

Maybe underestimation is—well, underestimated.
I mean, it's kind of nice not being expected to ever know shit.
But I worry that it's so nice
that the *Chicago Tribune* really gets to think
the Presidential library belongs there and not here because "With
no insult to Hawaii's respect for the life of the mind,
it's fair to say that very few people go there in fierce pursuit of
book learning."
And Adam Carolla really gets to dare us to name a single Hawaiian
who's ever done anything of significance, ever.
And Dave Chappelle really gets to tell us about pussy juice instead
of what it was like watching *12 Years a Slave.*

So if there's one good thing that's come out of this,
It's that I've learned not to hold back,
to confuse you by wearing a tat-baring muscle tee and motorcycle
boots
while I wax poetic about breath in Sanskrit mantra,
to let my students turn in essays to Dr. Kwon
hours before my band's next gig,
sip fine scotch after I finish teaching yoga,
and blush like a little girl when I fall in love.
And in return, I promise not to devalue you based on your look,

that I will not engage, will not prejudge, will not walk away
'til you open you mouth and show me your mind.

They say you'll never go broke underestimating the intelligence of
the American public,
and I say, not underestimating your intelligence gives me wealth.

And believe me, I am wealthy.

So I thank you for listening
and if you'll pardon me now,
I've gotta get up on the roof because
I hear the drinks are on the house.

All That Glitters Is Gold, or Why Paul Hamm Should've Given Up His Medal

Let me start by saying that it's not because I'm Korean
or that I don't play sports.
And it's not because I'm a traitor to my country,
my principles are out of whack,
or that I just need something to complain about,
but I think Paul Hamm should've given his medal back.
Now before you burn me at the stake,
I didn't say that the U.S. Olympic Committee strip it from him
or make him give it up.
I did say that he should give it back.
Why?
Because he didn't win.
The judges made a mistake,
admitted the mistake,
and despite the fact that in his heart he feels he earned the gold,
the numbers are there in black, white,
gold, bronze, and silver.
But then again, since when did anything on paper ever stop the U.S.
from taking what it wants?
If you ask Paul why he should keep the gold, he'll tell you
he did his job, and competed with pride and integrity.
Which I suppose means everyone else in the Olympics didn't.
All I keep hearing is how he's the victim, that he has to
"defend his medal,"
that he needs to make sure "his gold medal isn't stolen."
Like it's Korea causing the problem,
those damn Koreans making a fuss.
If it isn't nuclear arms, it's a gold medal,

and we sure as hell have to protect ourselves from any foreign attack
nucular, gymnastic, or otherwise.
And okay, so North and South Korea are two different countries,
but it's just a tiny little parallel that separates the two, you know,
and besides, now South Korea's got that anti-American president,
and everyone knows "anti-American" means "communist."
We might even need to seize all future Olympic Gold Medals
as a preemptive strike against any further monkey business like,
you know,
the truth.
All I have to say is turn the tables and see what a stink the U.S.
would've made if it were we who were cheated of the gold.
But that's not how it happened—
finders, keepers,
losers...winners?
And you know, I guess I shouldn't even be surprised,
because we got a long history of taking what doesn't belong to us.
Like Guam, the Hawaiian Kingdom, and the North American
continent.
Hell, the current presidency is based on taking what hadn't been
won.
But what I don't understand is how getting something for nothing
makes us the victims.
You know, just like we're victims of terrorism,
how we have to "defend our freedom,"
make sure that our "liberty isn't stolen" by,
oh,
declaring war on another country under false pretenses
and lying to the public while we send our brothers and sisters
to bleed for the Bush corporation.
I guess it doesn't matter
that millions were killed in Indonesia by a CIA-assisted coup in '65;
that we bombed the Dominican Republic during their elections in '66;
that we bombed Iran, Cambodia, Laos, Panama,

Somalia, Kuwait, Yugoslavia;

I mean who the hell did we not bomb?

And if we're not wiping out people,

we're hitting Vieques, Makua, and Bikini Atoll.

And some people wanna blame TV for all the violence in the world.

So you gotta forgive me if Paul Hamm got no portion of my

sympathy

in that Olympian controversy

because sometimes a medal is not just a medal.

Personally, I wouldn't want to keep something I didn't earn.

Every time I looked at that gold,

all I would think about is how much denial it takes

to say it's mine, all mine.

But I guess that's why I keep getting called a traitor to my country;

because if there's one thing Paul Hamm proved,

it's that stealing

is as American

as apple pie.

A Poem for Old Friends

These days, a lot of folks say, "40 is the new 30,"
which I realize is meant to be encouraging,
except it makes me wonder...

How different would things be if it had rained 30 days and nights?
If you tried to catch 30 winks of sleep?
If, whenever you had a squeaky door, you busted out your WD-30?
If, after the end of the Civil War, freed slaves were promised
30 acres and a mule?
If, *my day was going great and my soul was at ease*
until a group of brothers started bugging out
drinking the 30 oz?
Would Ali Baba have been as big of a hero if he had defeated
30 thieves?
Would Moses have gotten all ten commandments if he camped
Mount Sinai for 30 days and nights?
How many of the world's great pop artists would've gotten the
shaft if we only cared about *Music's Top 30?*

But I am not a 40s chauvinist.

I realize that most people would rather work a 30-hour week,
or rather have a sentence of 30 lashes of the whip,
that if a month were 40 days long, we'd get paid every 20 days
and it's hard enough for me to make my money last for those 15
as it is.

Still, the movie you laughed so hard at
was not called *The 30-Year-Old Virgin.*

See, I'm not so sure I want to go back.

My thirties were filled with bad dates, bad judgment,
bad budgeting, bad habits,
and my forties still are
but at least I know that now.
And on a good day,
I'll give you my top 40
I-am-woman, hear-me-roar
I've-looked-at-life-from-both-sides-now
I've-been-to-paradise-but-I've-never-been-to-me
reasons why 40 is better than 30.

(Though I will say when 20-somethings
hand me my change
and say *Thank you,* **ma'am**
I can't say a small, tiny, little part of me
doesn't want to smack 'em.)

Maybe when I'm 50, I'll be closer to hitting those
Power-of-Now,
radical-forgiveness,
relinquishing-the-ego,
abandonment-of-desire,
everything-is-impermanent,
all-enemies-are-gurus-in-disguise,
find-the-space-in-your-body-and-breathe
heights of evolution.

Until then, to those trying to console me
by saying 40 is the new 30:
I do appreciate the sentiment.
But if you say 40 is the new 30,
I say, don't push me back,
'cause I'm moving on.

Heart-Changing Medicine

*"I cannot explain this change of heart otherwise than by supposing
that when a Korean goes abroad, foreigners give him a certain
medicine to compass the change...refuse to take the heart changing
medicine, and come back to me soon unchanged in taste and dress."*
–a mother's letter to her son upon his departure for Hawai'i, 1897

The day you arrive, silk
clings to your skin and you
refuse to remove your stockings,
which you smooth with gloved hands.
In your husband's car,
you politely endure the heat,
your back straight while perspiration
licks Korea away.

Though he hands you a mu'u mu'u,
you draw from your suitcase
a pale blue hanbok, lined silver and white.
He insists you will be too hot,
says this is not Korea,
but you dress silently, methodically
for your first visit.

It is your first argument.

In proper colors,
you wade through plumeria and ginger
to what you believe will be
a mother-in-law's scorn.
Instead, you are surprised

by the sound of crying
from a brown-armed woman
grasping a memory recovered.

Tears mark clothes she has learned to wear,
and melt the distance
between then and now.
In the hot Nuʻuanu rains,
an old ajumeoni shakes her head
in gratitude
to the woman who has not yet taken
the heart-changing medicine.

White Horse Woman

The moment you snatch the picture
from her hand, her eyes widen
with understanding and implication.
To appease her you trade husbands,
give her the young, educated man
in exchange for the old, dark worker
waiting expectantly on the dock.
To you this twist of fate
meant less than preserving appearances—
a young girl's hysteria brought
jeopardy for the rest,
and what you do is less from love or care
than shrewdness and the understanding
of what it means to survive.
Over the years you both
bear three sons and a daughter.
As if to remind you of your tampering,
she caresses the cheek of
your daughter, my aunt,
whispers over and over
I should have been your mother.

Cane

On our drive to Kuilima
we pass fields of cane,
tall and sturdy, shifting in the breeze,
lovely hula hands
beckoning us to wander
among razor-sharp shoots.
Green rows promise
sweetness, Old Hawai'i,
but history and the six o'clock news
have taught us different.
In the fields lie missing persons,
recovered too late—
we learned early to hear ghosts
rustling deep among the stalks,
and we wondered as police
moved like workers in lines, searching,
if they too heard ghosts,
shaking cane in their anger.

Driving inland to Hale'iwa
I imagine roads you came to hate,
under a sun that burned the paper
of your already brown skin.
For you these fields meant
weary hands and a broken back,
laying track after track for a train
you'd never ride.
How many times did you dream of home
before digging up the picture
you kept of your youth,
to be creased and fluttering

in the hands of a bride?
And when she came to you,
did you understand
this white horse woman,
who made it your destiny
never to tame her?

Harabeoji,
you would never see my face,
though I would later trace
letters of your name
carved in weathered grey marble.
Deep into Waialua
is your weary gift to me—
the sight of these green fields
with longing and sadness,
built and wrought
from the labor of your years
as if one day to say, *Look*
to the child whose face presses on the window.

Smile

In the picture,
my father coaxes me to smile.
On his lap, I turn away from the lens,
my face twisted and angry
at the intrusion of a stranger's eye.
I don't remember the point of the outing,
or why it was we spent that Sunday
at the PX looking at cameras.
I do remember that he wouldn't give up.
Long after I'd made my intentions clear,
he gently took my chin in his hand
and turned it toward the camera,
sealing the moment
I would have otherwise forgotten.
In this picture,
my father is smiling next to a child
whose face is so sour,
the gazer must've pulled away
if only a little.

When you die,
I revisit you in pieces.
Looking at this photo,
I lose the years between,
feel your hand on my chin and your words in my ear,
yet am unexpectedly gifted
with what a stranger saw that day:
not a girl whose horror it was
to have an unwanted eye pierce her like a taunt,
but a father who loved his daughter so much
that the point was less to smile

than to simply testify we had spent one day together;
a Sunday we mistook
for countless among many,
rather than rare among few.
How can I not love
this Polaroid of my father?
I imagine the way you,
having erased my amateur tears,
must've held my hand as we leaned on the counter,
waiting expectantly
as darkness changed slowly
from a chemical swirl
into something both awkward and familiar.

New Year

Eventually it became only my mother's ritual.
We didn't ask where she was
on those particular mornings,
only knew her car filled with
anthuriums and birds of paradise
rolled down the Pali and toward Nuʻuanu.
Only she remembered the dead,
beginning each new year with the past,
with blood that didn't belong to her,
her hands crushing pots
into rain-soaked graves
of those who accused her, threatened her,
this woman from Korea.

One year it was my father's grave the rain muddied,
the year she made room
in the front seat for me.
We go to Nuʻuanu, Oʻahu,
clear weeds and brush dirt,
digging tiny pebbles out
from the grooves of lost names.
I ignore the guilt that whispers,
it's fear and not reverence
that guides my hands that follow my mother's.
We move slow in our ritual,
diligent in our craft.

My father's grave is the last stop.
Arriving at Punchbowl, I hum
the theme from *Hawaii Five-O*,
a gesture my mother forgives

as she counts columns and rows.
Each step we take is a wedge in our memory,
and our hands, side by side,
dance with weeds and stones.
The shiny bronze vase is clean
like a secret,
and though our hands touch,
my mother and I do not speak
in the comfort that comes
from the presence of stone.

My mother stops
to sit back on the grass,
oblivious to how I witness her languishing.
I want to ask if she regrets her life,
if there's a small part of her that welcomes the loneliness.
I think of how I used to hug her tight,
crushing her as if I could wring out the pain,
but for now she doesn't see that I am ready to leave,
only stares over mountains
into greying sky.
In the front seat of my mother's car
I watch her unfamiliar face
and pick at dirt beneath my nails
on this new year
without my father.

Homecoming

Already there are signs of my leaving,
with keys in hand and the empty glass
I rise to put away, only
she props her hands flat
on the tabletop, pushes herself
slowly upward as if
mirroring my own desires.
Behind her is the jar
of honey-colored tea
she will pour into my glass,
her way of saying *stay*
since we often cannot speak.
Silences will follow,
broken smiles and language
as I bury the questions deep,
exchange them for small utterances:
Gamsahamnida, Halmeoni
ne, ne.
Each year her sight grows weaker,
but she takes my hands close
examines the fingers,
the old, chipped polish.
Patting them softly
she speaks her words to me,
laughing at my confusion.
Hands not like you mom's,
then raises her own as if to show me
the pattern of my mother's life.
This is how we speak,
taking note of our connection
through hands, hair, eyes.

In me she searches for traces of herself,
to prove that we are not strangers,
though what she finds she never says.
Between us is the glass
I have always known,
the glass that meant vacations home
and visits to her apartment;
next to that, slices of persimmon.
This is what we hold:
the ritual of our dependence
that we are neither comfortable
performing nor neglecting.
In this comes tenderness
we cannot otherwise express—
the simple act of showing
that neither of us has forgotten.

Korea Halmeoni

We called her "Korea Halmeoni."

As if there were any other kind.

My father's mother was just "Halmeoni." On the outside, there were few differences; both were from Busan, both had Korean husbands, both came to Hawai'i. But Korea Halmeoni arrived much, much later. And by now, she has lived much, much longer.

When I enter her room, the first thing I see is her headset, which, since my last visit, seems to have gotten larger. I can hear the radio even before I approach her bed, choral sounds and conspiratorial hangeul streaming from the black foam cups. Her eyes are closed, having learned long ago they served no purpose. I wonder if she can feel my approach. The vibrations from her too-loud portable stereo have to outweigh my footfalls, but I still walk gently, hesitant, afraid of frightening her.

The outside world must be a constant surprise; her reality consists of Korean programs, three meals per day, sleeping, and forgetting the pain of aging. My hand on her knee, gently shaking her to signal my arrival, must feel like intrusion. Spontaneous, if not magic. Especially because she doesn't expect me. I'm her granddaughter, but she doesn't call me "uri adeul." I'm her daughter's child, not her son's. And we are strangers.

"Halmeoni," I say in a voice that feels too loud although I know she still has trouble hearing me. Her hands pull the headset from her ears and she tilts forward.

"Nuguseyo?"

"Brenda."

Her expression changes, a phenomenon whose oddness still amazes me because she cannot show me with her eyes what she feels, so the rest compensates. Her eyebrows lift, her mouth widens, and she nods slowly to tell me she understands who has come.

"Ah, Burenda wasseo?" She feels her way down to my hand, which she clasps in both of hers. They're dry and light, and if I decided to squeeze them, they would crumple like paper. "Tennkyu," she says, one of the phrases she'll speak in English.

"I brought cracker. You hungry?" I don't know the Korean word for cracker, and I can recognize the word for "hungry," but my mouth can't say it properly.

Not understanding, she leans toward me.

"Cracker," I repeat loudly. "You like?"

She still says nothing. In this moment, I know she feels as awkward as I do. The words fail, like always. I pull my hand out of her grasp and open the box of Ritz Crackers, moving quickly because I don't want her to interpret my motion as a rejection of her embrace. My fingers, unused to the swiftness with which I'm using them, tear the wax paper awkwardly. What matters here is the salty disc in my hand to show her what I cannot say, and the sooner I give it to her, the sooner she will see.

I press the Ritz into her palm. "Cracker. You like?"

The recognition is instant. She knows the feel of it, the ridged edges, the slightly oily texture, the bumps of salt on top.

"Oh, tenkkyu." Instead of taking the cracker with her fingers, she brings her palm upwards until her lips feel the Ritz's roughness and guides it into her mouth. She chews slowly, gratefully, to show me she appreciates my gift. This is the difference between us, I think. Each time I come here, she offers me what she has—slices of pear, yellow foil-wrapped coffee candies, macadamia nuts, shrimp crackers—but I refuse because I don't want them. Korea Halmeoni is not hungry, but she eats not to insult me. Her actions are driven by consideration and kindness; mine, desire and need.

I watch her finish what she holds in her hand, her chewing deliberate and rhythmic. There's no rush, nowhere to be, nothing to do next. Soon, the silence stretches a beat too long, so I pull another cracker from the wax-wrapped roll.

"You like?" I place it in her grasp.

She shakes her head. "No tenkkyu." Not missing a step, she says, "Burenda, put inside drawer."

This is one of the few moments I don't feel like a fraud, a failure. She has given me a task and I can follow through with obedience, something I'm vaguely aware indicates my respect for her, my recognition that I owe her something. In the third drawer of her dresser is an assortment of snacks, small treasures to fill her day. She isn't supposed to eat these things, and the nurses pretend she won't. The box I've brought is too big, so I take out the rolls and push them among half-filled bags sealed with twist-ties and cloth ribbons cut from old scarves.

When I sit beside her again, I put my hand out so that she can take it once more. She holds it with one, pats it with the other. I can feel the oil of the Ritz spread lightly over my skin. Eventually, her fingers travel to my rings. She squeezes the round hardness of the metal encasing my index finger, then moves to the bare skin of my ring finger. Finding nothing there, she squeezes anyway, maybe out of wishfulness, maybe out of admonition. I don't know. I know she worries. I know she would die peacefully if I had a husband, babies, things to ensure that I wouldn't end up alone, perhaps in a bed, with no one to visit me but disembodied voices coming through a headset.

I know what's coming.

"You get boyfriend?"

She waits expectantly for the answer she wants. But it doesn't come. I can't, not only because it isn't true, but because I can't explain. How can I explain to her? How can I say, *No, Halmeoni, I don't have a boyfriend. I see a man who fucks me and leaves, a man who makes me feel adored then disappears for days, a man I know is not right for me. It will all end soon, but he's here for now, and that's enough.*

I can't say it. And maybe she knows this as much as I.

When my boyfriend and I broke up, she said his name for months, asking my mother repeatedly why he never came around anymore, why we never married. I let her think it unraveled, that maybe we lost momentum having been together for so many years with no wedding, no ring. For her, his absence is the mystery of my life, the thing that won't make sense. It was easier to give her nothing, to let her form her own answers and blame the general unfairness of life. I don't know if she would have wanted the truth, to hear me say he lied, that there was another woman. That I don't love him anymore, that I'm glad he's gone. And she won't want to hear that I sleep with a man who wraps my heart in red wine, cigarette smoke, and long talks into the night. Whose arms engulf me as he sings love songs to me in Spanish, translating the words in the pause between lines. Who is not my boyfriend and whom I don't want to marry.

I know better than to think she hasn't felt heartbreak. I've long outgrown the narcissism of youth that believes the world only began with our births. But I still can't tell her. So instead, I make the same joke I've made for years now, the one whose brilliance lies in its complicity.

"No, Halmeoni. Trying."

She laughs merrily, her face erupting in lines and maps that texture her brown-spotted skin.

Pleased, she says, "Burenda, please eat more. You marry, okay?"

"Okay, Halmeoni. I eat more. I try get husband."

She pats my hand again because I've said the right thing. I'm not sure if she knows I'm lying, but maybe it doesn't matter. Maybe the semblance of compliance is enough.

And then the silence creeps in again. Her hand's motions over mine are steady, like a heartbeat. I wonder if she feels the stiffness in my posture because at best I see her once every four or five months now, and I have nothing to say.

One year ago, we thought she was going to die. She'd stopped eating, couldn't hold down water, and her small body, held taut over the years with defiance and shrewdness, deflated, lying in defeat under layers of blankets and quilts to ward off a chill that came from within.

"Brenda, go see Korea Halmeoni," my mother said when she called me at work. I rushed to the hospital to find a roomful of strangers circling the bed, asking in Korean who I was, why I was there. I couldn't answer, even as I suspected their questions. Finally, I blurted out that I was my mother's daughter, mistakenly thinking the secret word, "omma," would identify me. But the word failed. Without my mother there, I was nobody. Everyone has a mother. In the end, I was one body among many, and Korea Halmeoni had other things on her mind.

But she had things to say, too. For the next four days, I went to her a few hours each night, bearing a small tape recorder that I held close to her lips as she talked, and talked, about what, I didn't know. There are things she thought we should hear, things she needed us to remember, and I was the only one she would let save them. She took comfort in my ignorance. I couldn't react to her confessions. The only discomfort I felt was the weariness in my arm as the minutes passed and she wouldn't stop, as her voice grew weaker and crackled with gaps. Over four days, measured in clicks of the recorder telling me to replace the tape, she burst with language.

But she didn't die. Whatever pulled her away brought her back, and suddenly, there were the tapes to contend with. I hid them, knowing she wasn't ready for her secrets to be translated or heard. I hid them away so well that I now cannot find them.

Still, I know she hasn't forgotten them. She knows her words are somewhere in my apartment, probably lost among shoeboxes filled with objects of no use or folders stuffed with newspaper clippings and old essays. The tapes are the elephant between us, imaginary and uncomfortably present.

And now, there's nothing left to say.

The caresses across my hand try, but inevitably, she stops, then pats me three times.

"Burenda, you busy, yeah?"

"Yeah, Halmeoni. Plenty work."

"Oh." She pats my hand again. It should be routine by now, but it's not. "You go home. You work."

It's always this moment that I hate the most. I have to pull away from her, not because I'm replacing my hand with a cracker or putting snacks in the drawer, but because I'm leaving and neither one of us is sure when I'll return. I'm never quite convinced this isn't a test, if by staying and prolonging our silence, I will show her that I love her even though we know virtually nothing of each other, if I will prove to her that I am worthy of being uri adeul after all. Or if by leaving she will see that I understand her wish to let me go, accept her gift of not burdening me with our unease. Either way, there is only one thing to do.

"Okay, Halmeoni. You need something before I go?"

It's too much, too many words.

"Okay, bye-bye." She waves, nodding once.

I lean over to kiss her. "Bye, Halmeoni."

Her cheek is soft, and when I pull away, I imagine the imprint my lips left on her skin.

Before I can turn to leave, she has tugged the headset back on, muffling the sound of a man convincing her to do something I will never know.

The faint butter-like smell of Ritz crackers floats upward as I wave goodbye to Korea Halmeoni. I'm careful not to touch anything, else risk transferring the scent to the things I carry. I want to wash my hands, but it'll have to wait until I am home, a place Korea Halmeoni has never seen. A place where I have fulfilled my obligations. A place where family photos in dusty frames are enough. A place where, one day, unearthing what I've forgotten, I'll find her again.

Comfort Food

When I think about the year I spent in Korea, I think of how hard it was to eat.

Snapshot: I am meeting my Korean American boyfriend's Korean Korean mother for the first time. I expect that she will hate me because that's the way these things are supposed to go, but what I don't expect is the supreme level of insult I accidentally show her when she takes us to dinner at a small restaurant famous for its seafood stew and I decline the rich, mollusk-laden broth, asking my boyfriend how to pronounce the Korean word for "vegetarian." In his nervousness and anticipation of how much his mother will hate me, he has forgotten to tell her that I don't eat animals or animal products. A rapid blaze of Korean follows between them. Then, she looks at me from the side of her eyes, addresses me directly, jerks her chin in one harsh upswing, and continues to chew. I ask him what she said. He whispers, "She said, what, do you think you're going to live forever?"

Snapshot: I am eating alone in a country where people do not like to eat alone. And I am eating at a time—mid-afternoon—in a country where mid-afternoon is considered unacceptably late for lunch. The ajummas sitting at a table near the kitchen ignore me for ten minutes. Having been told that as much as 93 percent of communication is nonverbal, I hedge my bets that this is their way of saying that they will not feed me. But I am hungry, tired, and just a little bitchy, so I finally clear my throat and try to call out assertively, "Yeogi-yo"—"Over here!" They continue to talk. I clear my throat and call out again, intending to raise my volume only a little except the foreign words in my mouth trip me up and I end up yelling, "Yeogi-yo!" The ajummas stop. One of them—maybe the leader or maybe the one with the least power, I'm not sure—grudgingly walks over to me. I ask for mixed rice but with no meat.

It's a phrase I have practiced for days. But the ajumma doesn't understand me. Despite several hand motions—nonverbals, I think, use nonverbals—I finally find one combination that works: "Gogi?" then cross my forearms to create a large "X." The ajumma spits out, "Ttch," then turns around to tell the others what I was trying to say—I know because I recognize my mangled phrase coming out of her mouth in the way it's supposed to sound. They all begin to laugh and imitate me. Having never experienced such meanness, I'm too shocked to walk out, or tell them off, or overturn a table or break a window. Instead, I wait for my food and eat it quietly, poking around to make sure there is no malicious little bit of meat.

Snapshot: It's Ko-Yon-Jun, the annual games between rival universities Korea University and Yonsei. For three days, the schools compete at sports ranging from soccer to tennis to baseball. The competition is intense, but friendly, and the games are celebrated by massive drinking. I have been invited to a party hosted by Korea University's Swim Club held at a second-floor bar in Sinchon, a lively area full of bars, restaurants, and shops and whose main clientele are college students. Drinking is serious business in Korea, and having had more beer than I intended, I desperately scan the table full of food for something to eat. There is chicken, meat jeon, tteokbokki—a rice cake/seafood dish that all Koreans love—and finally, to my delight, a small platter of fried squid with celery and carrot sticks on the side. I load up my plate with veggies, and eagerly pop a carrot stick into my mouth...only to discover that it is not a carrot, but a hotdog sliced into a carrot stick-like shape. The celery, however, turns out to be celery. The diet of beer and celery is not enough to sober me up and I spend the next day in a fairly deep hangover.

Months before I left for Korea, I was terrified that there would be nothing for me to eat once I got to Seoul. It was a near obsession of mine. And nearly everyone laughed, patted me on the shoulder and said, "Don't worry—Asian food has lots of vegetables."

Which is true.

But what you don't discover until you get there is that the vegetables all come with meat. And contrary to what my meat-eating family believes, the soggy leaf of iceberg lettuce that's been sitting under the marinated chicken does not constitute an acceptable vegetarian meal.

For the first three weeks I was in Korea, I ate the same thing: kimbab—Korean sushi—and bibimbab—Korean mixed rice—with no meat. It was delicious. It was ostensibly vegetarian. But considering that I had a little less than a year to go, repeated meals of kimbab and bibimbab would not do. I developed a strange penchant for Pringles.

If you have never been to Korea, you might say, "Well, you don't have to eat Korean food. Get something else."

But you have to imagine that I considered this possibility. Then, you have to imagine that, if you have never been in Seoul, the restaurant market is based on one simple fact: Korean people like to eat Korean food. So you will see, on a typical street, dozens of restaurants—all Korean. In one area of Lotte World, one of the largest malls in Seoul, there are over twenty restaurants. All Korean, except one, which is Japanese (also vegetarian-unfriendly). The more casual food court is lined with stalls—all Korean. This is what it's like to eat in Seoul. There is the odd Italian restaurant here or there, and fast food: KFC, Pizza Hut, McDonald's, Krispy Kreme—but except for the latter, these cater to communal-meal carnivores, not lone vegetarians, and there is meat everywhere.

You also have to imagine that, contrary to what I realized was a predominant perception of Asians as smaller, healthier, vegetable-eating counterparts to their Western cousins, Asians like meat. Not only do they wholeheartedly subscribe to the belief that it makes one stronger; it's a sign of status. Vegetables are for monks and poor people. Anyone who's anyone eats meat.

After my third week in Korea, I thought, *Damn if I wasn't right. Unless I learn to subsist on a diet of kimbab, bibimbab, Pringles, and Krispy Kreme, I'm going to starve.*

And that's why I will never forget the day I found the Indian Café.

Truthfully, I had seen the large sign that said, "Indian Food" several times, but it never registered—being in Korea, my lens was trained to see what was unfamiliar—all things Korean—not what was familiar—all things I could get at home. But one day, feeling that if I ate another roll of kimbab I would have to commit a series of murders involving kimbab flagellation, I decided to cross the busy street toward the sign and face the long, dark, narrow stairway to the second floor, the kind of stairway that in a movie would have certainly led to a serial killer. I trudged forth, determined. At the top of the stairs, I pushed open a swinging glass door…and entered a quiet, dim but brightly decorated room whose tables were surrounded by multicolored scarves and saris, paintings, and images of Ganesh. A South Asian man with a kind face emerged from the kitchen to greet me in Korean, and when I said hello, he recognized the English-speaker in me and seated me in English, a lovely musical lilt to his accent. I was in heaven.

Even though it was the lunch rush, I was the only person there. Judging from the several cases of Hite beer in the corner, I suspected that their main clientele might be university students seeking out an exotic stop in a long night of drinking.

The man returned with a menu and a small glass of water. The menu was in English as well as Korean and boasted so many things familiar to my stomach—so many familiar vegetarian things. But at that moment, it wasn't the food I thought of. It was this man. I was so curious about what he was doing in Seoul, but that's not a question you ask someone right off the bat because you never know what that person's story is, so I swallowed my questions, and read the menu, returned to my hunger. My eyes roaming the page felt like a tongue licking a plate. And I chose my meal with a luxury I had not felt in a long time—the luxury of choice. Samosas, palak paneer, and garlic naan.

The food was delicious. The naan was not fluffy, but more like flatbread, and the taste of the samosas and palak paneer was more spicy than sweet. That these dishes were meant to be eaten family style and shared caused me no moment of hesitation. Alone in Seoul, I was my own family. I ate it all. I loved it. It reminded me of dinners with friends back home at our beloved Indian joints. And I relished the familiarity. For the first time, I truly understood the term "comfort food."

About halfway through my meal, an older Korean woman walked in. She had the slow movements and slight stoop of someone who spent most her life laboring, and one of those endearing grandmotherly smiles that makes you like someone right away. She said something to me that I couldn't understand, so I did what people generally do when this happens: I nodded and smiled. She seemed to be either the owner or the co-owner of the place, and after she checked on a few things, she shuffled over to the large TV near the side wall of the room and tuned in to a station of a man in a business suit standing in front of a white board and talking to a large group of people.

I guess what he said was pretty funny because not only was the audience laughing; she was, too. She kept turning around to look at me, the only other Korean person in the place, to share her laughter with me in that sweet way people do, but I had no idea what was being said, so I just kept smiling back at her between bites of naan and palak paneer. I hoped she didn't think I was being unfriendly.

The South Asian man was leaning against the counter, also watching the program, though he wasn't laughing, but observing dispassionately. I realized that he probably spoke Korean, or at least was much better at it than I was, and could follow along if not understand it completely. But each time the ajumma laughed, it was me she faced, not him.

And it was sometime during those ten minutes of her laughing at the TV that I started to feel the weight of the realization settling into my stomach to be digested with my palak paneer. I have heard people say the roots of culture are language and food. And there I was, in the country that, up until three generations ago, my bloodline called home, eating Indian food and completely oblivious to the sounds of Korean that filled the room. Thinking that this woman's family and my family had a shared history. That all it took was for her to look at my face and to feel we are kin. And so when she turned and spoke to me, her face buried in the breadth of her smile, for one moment, I wished more than anything that I had been born not in Hawai'i, but in Korea, so I wouldn't have had to say what I said next: "Mianhamnida. Miguk saram ye yo. Hangugeo jal mothamnida."

I'm sorry. I'm American. I don't speak Korean very well.

The smile remained on her face, though she looked a little confused.

"Oh," she said, then turned back to the television.

And I felt—as I did so many times that year—like a complete failure.

The South Asian man came from around the counter.

"Would you like some chai?" he asked me.

I nodded yes. And I sipped, tasting sweet, spice, and milk on my tongue, a flavor that felt strangely soothing, like the comforts of home.

Century's Lullaby

One hundred years ago,
Hawai'i was just a dream
of lush green fields of pineapple and sugar cane,
of warm trade winds licking dry your skin
damp with perspiration,
of sand that looked like cream dissolving beneath
the transparent blue waters separating
here and there,
Korea, Hawai'i,
this pacifying ocean
five years later separating
occupation and freedom,
beckoning for you to leave home
because home was burning in the rising sun,
home had lost the morning calm
and so you rode those waves
unsure if they were pulling you forward
or sucking you under
until they pitched you
to a rocky shore
where you planted your roots
in someone else's yard
bent double in the heat so strong and merciless,
you wondered how the rising sun so far away
could still singe you black on this tropical plain.

And one hundred years later,
Korea is my dream
of blue-mist mountains
and the smell of pine,
the insistent chanting of monks

and drum beats, of wooden beads,
long glinting spoons and silver chopsticks like jewelry
dipping into stone bowls of vegetables like
the colored ribbons of hanbok
as women spin in dance,
each turn a revolution back to tradition,
each rotation a recognition of Seoul,
this city of concrete and glass,
of marble floors and violins,
of cellular phones and subways snaking underground,
of neon red and pop music
and the steam of street vendors sheathed in plastic,
this city of excess and perpetual motion,
this city in which,
one hundred years later,
I cannot find you,
Harabeoji.

You died only months before my birth
meaning you were always theoretical,
the cord between us imagined,
braided by photographs of you,
photographs of me,
wishing I could cut and paste us together
if only to pretend we shared the same space
for one sacred flash of the camera,
you, the paper grandfather I would never meet,
I, the granddaughter you saw only through
the stretching flesh of my mother's belly,
time and her skin the things that kept us apart.

And as I walk these city streets,
I still feel time and my mother's belly flesh
encapsulating me from this place of my ancestry,

this place in which I do not belong,
this place in which i hanguk saram
do not recognize me,
call out to me in ilbon mal,
kon'nichiwa,
always surprised when I say,
aniyo, hanguk saram ye yo,
geurigo Hawai'i ae seo wasseoyo,
geureondae, hankuk saram ye yo,
to the vague suspicion
that perhaps I am confused or even refusing the truth.

Harabeoji,
hanguk saram ye yo,
but in this place of my ancestry,
this place in which,
one hundred years later
I can find no trace of you,
my blood is theory,
my home, time and the flesh of my mother's belly,
my home in someone else's yard
the product of this country's rape,
and so you see why I find it ironic
when asked
ilbon saram ye yo?
because, in truth, maybe I am a child born of the rising sun,
or at the very least, its shadow.

But Harabeoji,
hanguk saram ye yo.
tell me,
hanguk saram ye yo.

Because just as I fought to see your face,
one hundred years later,

I will escape the skin that keeps me from you,
leave familiar walls to labor through
passageways into this place of your birth,
this city of strangeness,
this city estranged,
until I hear it call me hanguk saram,
until I feel it embrace my foreign birth
until I feel your hands cradle my infant head—

hours of innocence
in the morning calm.

Remembering the Pieces

To gain form, one must break. To make a statue, the sculptor requires that the stone sacrifice its pieces. Rock falls away, but its presence remains. Absence creates the image; we see in equal parts what is there and what is not. Space embraces matter, giving it outline, shape, dimension, texture, and the figure thanks its fragments' ghosts.

On a dusty road in Kyongju, my mother and I hike into South Mountain, what our guide calls "the temple without walls." We don't go very far into the woods, but even a few steps are enough to show us the miracle of this place: each rock wears carvings of buddhas and pagodas, many of them over a thousand years old. Peering through leaves, they wait like wise men, their stillness grounded in something deeper than stone.

The first turn leads to an open area with a cluster of large, flat boulders nestled against several buddhas standing near. Our driver says something to my mother, then bows down before a small altar placed near them. I watch him prostrate himself three times as I ask my mother what he has said.

"This is the most sacred place in Korea. He said we should pray."

The guide points to the boulders and tells me that in the middle is a space believed to be the opening through which the mountain's spirits travel. During the Japanese occupation, foreign soldiers assaulted this place, thrusting a log deep into the hole.

The log stayed there for decades until the time came for Koreans to reclaim her, casting off the offender in a brilliant shower of splinters.

There are no traces, but she wears the memory like a faded scar.

When we walk the streets of Seoul, well-meaning vendors call out, "Kon'nichi wa," much to my confusion. My mother explains that I look different, that my foreignness shows in my clothes, my walk, is detectable in my gestures, my gaze. The idea of a Korean so far removed is odd, so they make the default assumption: that I'm Japanese.

But my mother is different. She has learned the art of context, so her tongue and body remember what they must do. No one here thinks she's American, just as no one in Hawai'i thinks she's an immigrant. For her, this is coming home. And so I stay near, if only to remind myself that I belong.

I quickly learn that proximity doesn't guarantee reception. Browsing through the open market in Jeju-do, we meet a vendor who sells therapeutic seed oil. I watch his demonstration of the machine that crushes a mix of sesame, flax, and other things, then extracts the honey-brown liquid into a plastic bottle. My mother translates his pitch. As we discuss how many bottles to buy, I notice the vendor's small daughter has come out from behind the stand to stare at me. Her mouth is open as she watches me talk. I smile and wave, but she doesn't move. The vendor says something and my mother laughs. The little girl has never seen a Korean speak only English.

It occurs to me that to her I am somewhat of a freak, a source of amazement, perhaps, but mostly shock.

And I still keep close to my mother. If I stand near enough, maybe they will see our resemblance after all—that we are, in fact, connected.

Back at the hotel, we turn on the television; I'd forgotten that today is June 15, that North and South Korea will meet for the historic summit, sit side-by-side to discuss reunification. My mother jokes that every time I come to Korea, something monumental happens. That last time I was here, the first man walked on the moon.

On screen, thousands of hanbok-clad women jump up and down frantically, waving and welcoming Kim Dae Jung. Something about this seizes me because I can't understand the desperation behind the joy, how their bodies don't weary from such feverish displays of happiness. The next day, our guide takes a more cynical view—she reads their gestures as articulated, manipulative, seducing their witnesses.

Perhaps after centuries of attack, we have learned that pleasing the enemy procures power.

She doesn't believe reunification will happen. Neither does our driver. I feel falsely idealistic; they must know something I don't. The television's images come wrapped in unfamiliar words. I can see the faces, but voices elude me. Maybe the eyes are not enough—a picture minus its thousand words.

I promise myself that I'll return once I've learned the language. I'm not really sure when that'll be, but it's one of those indefinite definites—a matter of time.

Weeks after coming home to Hawai'i, I still find the island somewhat peculiar. Nothing looks quite right anymore. It's as if Korea has formed a template in my mind and my surroundings refuse to match. The day I get my pictures developed, I lay them out on the carpet, where they form a long chain of moments, captured images that squeeze themselves happily into the pattern of memory. Yet somehow, the photos themselves aren't enough. My fear of losing the connective tissue between each image is so strong that I pore over the pages of the journal I took to Korea, inserting text, cementing with words what my mind might forget.

There is one picture that I can't put down, let go, or commit to memory: a lotus painted on the pillar next to the gong at Chogaesa temple in Seoul. Eventually, I separate this one from the stack because my constant need to see it has resulted in bent corners and smudged fingerprints on the rest. After I'd passed my second qualifying exams in Los Angeles, I'd gotten a tattoo of a lotus bud, its leaves closed and waiting. But this one is open, in full bloom, and one week later, I have an appointment with a tattoo artist whose specialty includes cover-ups.

As she dips her needle into the ink, she asks me why I want this lotus instead. I tell her that I've had enough of anticipation, that it's time to reach my potential. She laughs. I tell her about my trip to Korea and where I found the image. She wants me to get it blessed, especially because it came from a temple. When I ask her why, she says, "Because it's part of you now. You don't want to steal it. Ask permission, then it'll be yours."

I don't know where to go, who will help me. I'm not a Buddhist and I feel like a fraud. So I visit a healer who places her hands over my skin. For a brief second, there is pain, the flesh remembering trauma. But this soon gives way to heat, warmth, and the gentle feel of one person touching another.

Knowing how much I miss Korea, my mother takes me to Mu-Ryang-Sa in Pālolo Valley. In Korea, I saw temple upon temple, old and faded, a testament to survival. Pulling up to this one, I'm unprepared for the bright colors and sharp outlines, how clearly I can see the lotus at the edge of each beam.

Properly entering the grounds, we pass through the Gate of the Four Heavenly Kings. Representing East, West, South, and North, they guard against the demons that we find within, things that destroy us, like greed and pride. The guardians in Korea dressed in colors whose brilliance were memory, yet these are new; I see how their eyes discourage impurity, how tightly their hands grip their monsters. The glowing blue demon looks more enslaved, just as detailed scales make their dragons writhe. Walking among kings, we leave behind the everyday world.

Straight ahead is the peace pagoda, a replica of Sokka-Tap in Kyongju. To the left, the stone brother of the buddha Miruk Bosal Sang in Korea's National Museum. To the right, the likeness of Korea's oldest bell, Emille, beckoning all to enlightenment. If it's possible to be in two places at once, then this is what I feel seeing Korea's twin. I know that we are still in Hawai'i. I know that this is not Korea. But the buddha, pagoda, and bell feel like home.

Mu-Ryang-Sa means "Broken Ridge Temple." When they first built the main hall, the roof exceeded legal height limitations. To remedy the error, they broke the hall's roof.

Inside Great Hero Hall, I am learning to breathe. With each exhale, the world falls away. Our teacher tells us to experience the world free of naming. Language forms thought, and thought, judgment. Each time words enter my mind, I let them go. This lets me focus on the soft rumble within as air enters my lungs, the tiny pain when they fill to capacity, the initial push as the air escapes. Several breaths later, all I feel is air; my skin grows thinner and disappears as I slowly open to all sound and perception.

To reach enlightenment, we shatter the self.
By fragmenting we break what holds us apart.
All is impermanent; all this will pass.
In each incarnation, we are the sum of our breathing.

Inhale, exhale, inhale, exhale, north, south, inhale, exhale.
Inhale, exhale, inhale, exhale, here, there, inhale, exhale.
Inhale, exhale, inhale exhale.
inhaleexhale.
inhaleexhale

XXX

Buddha in L.A.

Late on a Thursday afternoon,
Buddha travels west on the 10 Freeway
in the slow lane.
The red Honda merging from La Cienega
follows him for a moment,
but perhaps unnerved by that
impeccably serene smile,
zips to the left and disappears.
I think most of us would prefer that he face forward.
But there is something about that large golden head,
those smooth shoulders,
the concealed nipple that makes me pull
one lane closer.
I wonder where he will go.
North to Malibu?
West to Santa Monica?
Robertson to Beverly Hills?
At the 405 interchange,
this passenger of two Asian boys
changes lanes and heads south,
curving up and around us before disappearing.
Had I not gone west,
I would have seen how
the setting sun
touched his face for a moment
kissing it softly in thanks
before he rolled to a stop,
caught in gridlock.

Author's Note

According to yogic tradition, we are given a particular number of breaths in each lifetime, and when we reach that number, we come to the end of our current existence. The practice of pranayama or breathwork, then, is about controlling the breath and cultivating greater life energy. Because the word for "breath" in Hangeul is "sum," the title of the collection is both a play on the word "breath" in Korean as well as a reference to the idea that at any given moment, we are the total of our breaths thus far.

As an exploration of this idea, Stephanie Chang's artwork for the section dividers is a blend of Sanskrit, Hangeul, and mudra, and came together after a discussion we had about the ways in which language, breath, and the body mirror each other. Sanskrit is a vibrational language, and each letter resonates with particular chakras or energy centers in the body. Its semivowels form mantras for the first four chakras—lam (1st chakra, root), vam (2nd chakra, sex), ram (3rd chakra, navel), and yam (4th chakra, heart)—each connected to different aspects of our evolution. The Hangeul on each page translates to an interpretation of the particular chakra, representing foundation, desire, self-empowerment, and love, respectively, and the sections have been ordered according to theme rather than chakra order. The emphasis on Sanskrit comes from the understanding of it as the language of breath. My teacher Dharma Widmann says that in order to correctly pronounce the words, one must aspirate precisely. It is an incredibly physical language, with the tongue dancing in five positions: gutteral, palatal, cerebral, dental, and labial. Considered a "pure language," its utterance is said to bring us the clarity necessary for understanding our true nature.

Acknowledgements

Deepest thanks to everyone at Bamboo Ridge Press, especially Darrell Lum and Eric Chock for helping me to shape this book and to see bridges where there were gullies; Joy Kobayashi-Cintrón and Gail Harada for knowing how to balance optimism and realism as well as their expertise when it came time to move into production, and Wing Tek Lum for his constant support and gentle scolding whenever I needed it. I am also indebted to the Bamboo Ridge writing group for the many nights of thoughtful critique and vegetarian potlucks; Normie Salvador, Don Wallace, and Karen Iwamoto for their sharp eyes during the many stages of the editing process; Muriel Fujii and Brett Kelly for their photographic 9-1-1; Annie Koh for our lunches at Peace Café and her transliterations of the Korean words and phrases here; and Stephanie Chang, for intuitively finding a way to express with images the very ideas I could only conceptualize in words. I'm humbled and honored by the encouragement of Nora Keller, Elaine Kim, Don Lee, Russell Leong, Zack Linmark, Chris McKinney, Gary Pak, Ishle Yi Park, Cathy Song, and Kathryn Waddell Takara, and my warmest aloha goes out to my beloved tribe of slam poets, in particular Travis Thompson and Cawa Tran. In my heart are all the friends and family whose love was the thread allowing me to stitch together the moments of my life—there are too many to name here, and I hope they know how grateful I am—and a special gamsahamnida goes to Joyce and Victor Lee, Leslie Oyama, Anjali Puri, Brian Bilsky, Dawn Sanderson, Lesley Ueoka Fronjian, Ruth Huang, my bandmates, and the Open Space Yoga ohana. Lastly, I would like to thank King-Kok Cheung for her unending belief in me, and Alex Trent Handler for refusing to let me forget that I promised I would one day bring this project to completion.

About The Author

Brenda Kwon is the author of *Beyond Keʻeaumoku: Koreans, Nationalism, and Local Culture in Hawaiʻi,* and co-editor of *YOBO: Korean American Writing in Hawaiʻi.* Her works have appeared in various journals and anthologies, and she has performed her poetry in Honolulu, New York, Los Angeles, Boston, and Seoul. A 2005 Fulbright Fellow, she lives in Honolulu, where she teaches writing and yoga, and plays music with her band.